BW Extreme Closeup Tulips of the Netherlands 24 in the Art in Flowers Special Collection of William Robert Stanek

robertstanek.pictorem.com

August Rains

A Story of Love, Memory, &
the School That Shaped a Town

By Robert Stanek

This is a work of fiction. All the characters, names, places, and events portrayed in this book either are products of the author's imagination or are used fictitiously. Any resemblance to any actual locale, person, or event is entirely coincidental.

August Rains

A Story of Love, Memory, & the School That Shaped a Town

robert-stanek.com

Acknowledgments

I would like to thank my writing group, my editors, and my publishers for their many years of support. A writer can't survive in this business without such wonderful support. I want to personally thank Jeannie, Tony, Frank, Ed & Holly, Patrick, Susan and everyone else who supported the journey and kept me on track with the writing. Your insights and assistance have always been much appreciated. I also want to thank Will, Jasmine, and Sapphire for always being the first readers to devour my work and come back hungry for more.

Dedication

For the teachers who shape us,
the students who inspire us,
and the communities that carry us forward.

Epigraph

"Autumn shows us how beautiful it is to let things go."

—Unknown

Table of Contents

ACKNOWLEDGMENTS 6

DEDICATION 7

EPIGRAPH 8

TABLE OF CONTENTS 9

AUTHOR'S NOTE 13

PROLOGUE 15

THE NEW GUY IN THE HALLS 19

WHEN MUSIC FLOATED THROUGH THE WALLS 23

A TEACHER'S WORST NIGHTMARE: PIANO PRACTICE 27

SING IT LOUD, ANGELICA! 31

TEAMWORK MAKES THE CONCERT WORK 35

A STANDING OVATION FOR MISS ANGELICA 40

SECRETS OVER COFFEE 44

LEAVES AND LESSONS 49

A QUESTION OF COURAGE 53

A NIGHT TO REMEMBER 56

A RING, A PIANO, AND A QUESTION 61

HAPPILY EVER AFTER, SCHOOL EDITION 65

LITTLE BOBBY, BIG DREAMS 69

TOM'S TEST BLUES 73

PROGRESS? NOT ON MY WATCH! 77

MUSIC BRINGS THE TOWN TOGETHER 85

PRINCIPAL ANDERSON HAS ENTERED THE CHAT 94

SUMMER SERENADES 102

LIVING IN A SHADOW 110

STORM CLOUDS AND SILVER LININGS 115

A QUIET EVENING AT HOME 124

GOODBYE, BOBBY, HELLO WORLD 133

THE NAM CALLS BOBBY 137

THE DIAGNOSIS THAT CHANGED EVERYTHING 145

ONE LAST CHRISTMAS AT SCHOOL 149

HER LAST LESSON 153

TOM THE JANITOR, TOM THE FRIEND 160

A NOTE LEFT UNPLAYED 164

THE NEW YEAR'S RETURN 167

BOBBY'S SONG 172

SPRING'S WHISPER 176

THE FIRST DROPS OF RAIN 180

A VISIT AND A REMINDER 184

THE FIGHT FOR JANE'S SCHOOL 189

TOM'S SHADOW RETURNS 194

A CALLS TO ARMS 197

THE LAST DAY 202

GOODBYES IN THE GYM 206

PROGRESS VS. NOSTALGIA: THE DEBATE 210

A PICTURE WORTH A THOUSAND MEMORIES 214

AN EVENING OF TEARS AND TRIBUTES 218

THE STORM OUTSIDE, THE CALM WITHIN 225

LIGHTNING STRIKES (METAPHORICALLY) 229

THE MORNING AFTER 232

LESSONS FROM THE MAPLES 236

TOM'S OUTSTRETCHED HAND 240

LOCKING THE PAST AWAY 243

HOMEMADE CINNAMON ROLLS 246

FOR TOMORROW: A SONG FOUND 251

PLAYGROUNDS DON'T LAUGH ANYMORE 254

A JOURNEY TO INDIANA 257

A NOTE AND A MEETING 262

LETTING GO 267

ONE LAST WALK THROUGH TIME 271

POT ROAST AND NEW BEGINNINGS 275

AROUND THE LAKE AND TO THE TABLE 278

A SKY WASHED CLEAN 282

ROOTS IN HER HONOR 286

DEAR ANGELICA... 289

PIRATES, ROAST CHICKEN, AND FAMILY FEELS 292

AUTUMN'S GENTLE GOODBYE 296

ABOUT THE AUTHOR 306

Author's Note

When I first wrote *August Rains* as a short story, it was a quiet reflection on memory, love, and change. At the time, I didn't realize the depth of the themes waiting to be uncovered. As I expanded it into a novel, it became much more—a story about resilience, legacy, and the courage to embrace what comes next.

John Anderson's journey is deeply personal to me, as I imagine it will be for many readers. It is a tribute to those who dedicate their lives to others—the teachers, mentors, and community builders who leave lasting imprints on the world around them. Through John's reflections, his connection to Angelica, and the bonds he forms with people like Tom and Cindy, *August Rains* reminds us that while some chapters close, the heart of what we create endures.

Thank you for joining John on his journey. I hope his story brings you the same peace and perspective it brought me as I wrote it.

—Robert Stanek

Prologue

John Anderson paused in the empty hallway, his hand brushing against the cold steel of the lockers as he leaned slightly on the wall. Through the wide front windows of the school, the two great maples came into view, their branches bending slightly in the crisp October wind.

The afternoon sun dipped low, casting long, golden rays over the schoolyard. The leaves on the maples were in their full autumn splendor, a riot of fiery reds, rich golds, and warm browns. A gust of wind caught the branches, sending a flurry of leaves spiraling down like confetti.

For a moment, John simply watched, his chest tightening with an emotion he couldn't immediately name.

The leaves tumbled lazily through the air, some coming to rest on the cracked asphalt of the playground, while others clung stubbornly to the branches. Each gust shook more free, scattering them in unpredictable arcs.

It reminded him of his first day at Jane's School, standing in this very spot, marveling at the same maples. They'd been younger trees then, their trunks thinner, their branches less expansive. He could still remember the sound of children's laughter outside as he'd adjusted his tie and prepared himself to face his first classroom.

How quickly the years had passed.

Now, the playground was empty, the swings creaking slightly in the breeze. The laughter was gone, replaced by silence, save for the occasional whisper of the wind.

John rubbed his hands together, the chill from the old school's drafty hallways seeping into his skin. The falling leaves seemed to echo his thoughts—beautiful, but fleeting. Each one, a symbol of time slipping away.

He thought of the seasons he'd watched unfold from this very window: spring's blossoms, summer's lush greenery, winter's stark, skeletal branches. Autumn, though, had always been his favorite. It was a time of change, of endings and beginnings, when the world seemed to hold its breath before the long sleep of winter.

A single leaf, vibrant red and perfectly shaped, caught on the windowpane in front of him. He reached out, his fingertips brushing the cold glass. It reminded him of a moment with Angelica, years ago, as they'd walked together under these very trees.

"What's your favorite season?" she'd asked him.

"Spring, I suppose," he'd said without much thought. "A time for growth."

She'd laughed then, a light, musical sound. "Not me. I love autumn. It's honest—things end, but it's beautiful, don't you think? Like it's promising you that endings aren't so bad after all."

He hadn't understood her then, not fully. But now, standing in the quiet hallway with the weight of the years behind him, her words resonated.

The creak of the door behind him broke his reverie. Turning, he saw Tom Ferillo step into the hallway, his work boots scuffing lightly against the linoleum.

"Mr. Anderson," Tom said, his tone uncertain. "Everything all right?"

John nodded, clearing his throat. "Just… watching the leaves."

Tom followed his gaze to the maples outside. "They're something, aren't they? Cindy says we should take the kids to rake some up this weekend. Let them jump in the piles like we used to."

John's lips curved into a faint smile. "That's a good idea. Let them enjoy it while they can."

Tom hesitated, then said, "Those trees… they've been here longer than either of us, haven't they?"

"They have," John replied. "I sometimes think they've seen more than we ever will."

Tom chuckled softly. "Maybe. They'll still be here when we're long gone, though."

"Perhaps," John said, his voice quiet. "But even trees have their seasons."

The two men stood in companionable silence for a moment, watching as another gust sent more leaves scattering across the schoolyard.

Finally, John pushed off the wall, his hand brushing the lockers one last time. "Better get moving. These halls won't clean themselves."

Tom nodded. "And I've got to lock up soon. You sure you're all right, Mr. Anderson?"

John glanced back at the maples, their branches stretching toward the sky as if reaching for something just out of grasp.

"I'll be fine, Tom," he said. "It's just the season. It always makes you think, doesn't it?"

Tom smiled faintly. "It does."

As John turned to leave, he took one last look at the window and the red leaf still clinging there. Angelica had been right. Endings weren't so bad, not when they could be as beautiful as this.

The New Guy in the Halls

1957

The brisk autumn air greeted John Anderson as he stepped out of his rust-speckled Chevrolet, the engine coughing twice before quieting altogether. Jane's School loomed ahead of him, a sturdy red-brick building with ivy clinging to its weathered facade. The morning sun caught the frost still clinging to the grass, giving the schoolyard a crisp shimmer. Two great maples framed the entrance, their fiery leaves fluttering lazily in the light breeze, promising to carpet the ground with color as the season deepened.

John adjusted his tie, a slightly-too-wide brown number gifted by his father, and tugged at the worn leather strap of his satchel. This was it—his first day as a full-time teacher. A mixture of nerves and excitement twisted in his stomach, a feeling he hadn't experienced since boarding a troop train during the war. This time, however, he wasn't marching toward chaos; he was walking toward opportunity.

The schoolyard was alive with energy. Children in hand-me-down coats and scuffed shoes darted around, their laughter piercing the morning air. A boy chased a girl with a paper airplane, the delicate craft banking sharply before plummeting into a pile of leaves. Nearby, two girls huddled over a jump rope, counting off in sing-song voices as they took turns.

John paused just inside the gate, his fingers brushing against the wrought iron. He had been here two days prior for orientation, but the building had been quiet then, empty save for the principal and a few staff members. Today, it was as if the school itself had come to life, humming with purpose.

A tall man in a charcoal suit and wire-rimmed glasses emerged from the front doors. Principal Harrison. He spotted John and raised a hand in greeting.

"Mr. Anderson! Glad to see you've made it. Quite a day to start, eh?"

"Yes, sir," John replied, stepping forward with a handshake. "It's a fine morning."

Principal Harrison clapped him on the shoulder. "The first day's always a whirlwind. But don't worry, you'll find your rhythm soon enough. The fourth-grade room is just down the main hall on the left. Got your keys?"

John patted his pocket and nodded. "Yes, sir. I'll head in now."

"Good man. Oh, and don't let the noise overwhelm you. It's a lively bunch."

As Harrison moved off to greet another teacher, John turned his attention to the building itself. He hesitated briefly at the threshold before stepping inside. The familiar scent of chalk dust and floor polish enveloped him immediately, tugging at a memory of his own schooldays—a time when the world felt big and brimming with possibilities.

The hallway stretched before him, lined with steel lockers painted an institutional green that had seen better days. Each was slightly dented or scratched, bearing the marks of generations of students. Paper decorations adorned the walls, and posters with cheerful slogans like *"Reach for the Stars!"* were tacked up with precision.

Children moved past him in small, chattering groups, some casting curious glances at the new teacher. John smiled politely, though his heart thudded in his chest. He was sure he looked out of place, an untested young man in a sea of confident routines.

"Excuse me," came a small voice. John turned to see a girl of about nine, clutching a stack of books almost as tall as she was. "Are you the new fourth-grade teacher?"

"I am," John said, kneeling slightly to meet her gaze. "Mr. Anderson. And you are?"

"Clara Mayfield," she said with a shy smile. "Mrs. Jennings said we're supposed to make you feel welcome."

"Well, you're doing an excellent job, Clara. Thank you."

The girl giggled and hurried off, leaving John with a small sense of reassurance.

Reaching his classroom, John unlocked the door and pushed it open. Inside, rows of wooden desks stood ready, their surfaces marked with the carvings and scratches of previous occupants. A chalkboard spanned the far wall, already bearing a welcoming message written in careful, looping script: *Welcome to Fourth Grade!*

Setting his satchel on the desk, John allowed himself a moment to absorb it all. This room, this day—it was the beginning of something. The weight of responsibility pressed gently on his shoulders, but so did the thrill of possibility.

Somewhere down the hall, a piano began to play. The soft, melodic notes drifted toward him, threading through the faint din of the school. A teacher humming along, he guessed, though the sound was unexpected. It wasn't part of the orderly rhythm he'd imagined for the day.

John glanced toward the door, tempted to investigate, but he stayed put. There would be time enough to meet the others. For now, he had a classroom to prepare.

"Here we go," he murmured to himself, straightening a desk. His teaching career had officially begun.

When Music Floated Through the Walls

The faint strains of piano music reached John's ears as he reviewed his lesson plan at his desk. It was soft at first, a delicate melody threading its way through the usual hum of the school—a child crying, lockers slamming, and footsteps echoing in the halls. He paused, his pencil hovering above the notebook.

Music? He hadn't been told there was a music program.

A sudden, bright laugh startled him from his thoughts. It came from down the hall, followed by a burst of youthful giggles and a woman's voice—gentle yet commanding. John frowned. The noise was disruptive, spilling into his classroom and stealing the attention he'd tried so hard to maintain with his fourth graders during the morning's lesson.

Setting down his pencil, John stood and adjusted his tie. He stepped out into the hallway, where the music was now accompanied by a sing-song voice leading a chorus of children.

"If you're happy and you know it, clap your hands…"

John moved toward the source of the sound, his polished shoes tapping steadily against the linoleum floor. The music room door was ajar, and through the crack, he caught a glimpse of a woman seated at a shiny black piano.

She was young, likely in her mid-twenties, with auburn hair swept into a loose bun. She leaned slightly forward as she played, her posture poised yet relaxed. A group of children stood around her, their small hands clapping in unison as they sang, their faces alight with joy.

The woman stopped playing and clapped along with them, laughing as one of the boys tried to keep up. "Almost there, Charlie! You'll get it by the end of the week."

John cleared his throat loudly, more out of habit than necessity. The music and laughter ceased instantly, and the children turned toward the door. The woman followed their gazes and smiled, her green eyes warm and inviting.

"Well, hello there!" she said, rising from the piano bench. Her voice was melodious, as if the music hadn't left her even in speech. "You must be the new fourth-grade teacher."

"I am," John said, taking a hesitant step inside. "John Anderson."

"Angelica Thompson," she replied, brushing her hands against her skirt before extending one toward him. Her handshake was firm but unhurried, her smile unwavering. "I'm the new music teacher."

"That explains the piano," John said, nodding toward the gleaming instrument. "I wasn't aware the school had one. It's, uh… quite the surprise."

"Good surprise or bad surprise?" Angelica asked, tilting her head with a playful glint in her eye.

John hesitated. "I suppose that depends on how much my students enjoy the distraction."

The children giggled, sensing a hint of teasing in his tone. Angelica laughed lightly. "Distraction? Music is hardly a distraction, Mr. Anderson. It's an enhancement! Studies show that engaging with music improves concentration and cognitive development."

"I see," John said, though he didn't entirely. He folded his hands behind his back, trying to reconcile this spirited new colleague with the quiet, orderly environment he had envisioned for his classroom.

Angelica gestured to the children. "All right, everyone, back to your seats. Recess is almost over."

The children scurried to gather their things, filing out with a chorus of goodbyes directed at Angelica and curious glances cast at John.

As the last child left the room, Angelica perched on the edge of the piano bench, her fingers idly brushing the keys. "I'm guessing you're not much of a music person, Mr. Anderson."

John shifted his weight. "I appreciate music as much as anyone, Miss Thompson. I simply prefer it doesn't disrupt my classroom."

"Fair enough," she said with a slight nod. Then, leaning conspiratorially, she added, "But give it time. The kids love it, and I suspect you might, too, once you see what it brings out in them."

"I'll take that under advisement," John said, though his tone was softer than before.

Angelica smiled again, rising from the bench. "Well, don't let me keep you. I'm sure you have important fourth-grade lessons to plan."

"Indeed," John replied, stepping back toward the door. "Welcome to Jane's School, Miss Thompson. I hope you find it… agreeable."

"Oh, I will," she said brightly. "And I hope you'll find a way to stop by again, perhaps when the kids are singing in full harmony."

John gave her a polite nod and left the room, the faint sound of her humming following him down the hall. As he returned to his classroom, he couldn't shake the feeling that something about Angelica Thompson wasn't just new—it was transformative. Whether that was a good or bad thing, he wasn't yet sure.

A Teacher's Worst Nightmare: Piano Practice

John stood at the front of his fourth-grade classroom, chalk in hand, carefully writing out a sentence diagram on the blackboard. Behind him, the murmur of pencils scratching against paper suggested that his students were, for the moment, focused.

"Now, who can tell me the subject of this sentence?" he asked, turning to face the room.

A few hands went up, and John nodded toward Clara Mayfield, who sat in the front row.

"'The cat chased the mouse,'" Clara recited. "The subject is 'cat.'"

"Very good," John said, allowing himself a small smile. "And the predicate—"

The faint sound of piano music drifted into the room, soft and lilting at first. John's words faltered. He glanced toward the closed door, where the muffled melody began to grow louder, a cascade of playful arpeggios.

The class stirred, students exchanging glances as the music seeped in. A few heads turned toward the windows, as though searching for the source.

"Eyes up front," John said firmly, though the distraction had taken hold. "The predicate. Who can tell me?"

The piano launched into a jaunty, upbeat tune, accompanied by bursts of singing voices: *"Row, row, row your boat…"*

A ripple of laughter spread through the classroom.

"Settle down," John said, his voice sharp enough to pull the children's attention back, if only briefly. "Now, about the predicate—"

The song reached a crescendo, and the children began humming along under their breath. Clara started tapping her pencil against her desk in time with the rhythm. Tommy Wilkes swayed slightly in his chair.

John set the chalk on the ledge with an audible click. "Everyone, pencils down. Clara, Tommy, enough of that. Focus."

His words were drowned out by the second verse, this time harmonized. John's jaw tightened. He strode to the door, opened it just enough to poke his head out, and followed the sound to the music room.

There, Angelica was at the piano, her fingers dancing across the keys as she guided the children through the song. A dozen students stood around her, swaying and clapping in perfect time, their voices carrying effortlessly into the hall.

"Okay, everyone!" Angelica called brightly, finishing with a flourish. "One more time, and let's really make it ring!"

John stepped into the room, his presence cutting through the cheerful noise. "Excuse me, Miss Thompson."

The students turned in unison, their singing halting abruptly. Angelica looked up, her hands hovering over the keys. "Mr. Anderson! What a surprise. Care to join us?"

"I'm afraid I can't," John replied evenly, though his tone carried a hint of tension. "I'm in the middle of a lesson, and the sound is... carrying into my classroom."

Angelica straightened, brushing her hands over her skirt. "Oh, I see. My apologies. I didn't realize the music would travel so far."

"It does," John said, folding his hands behind his back. "Quite clearly, in fact."

The children exchanged wide-eyed glances, sensing the shift in tone.

Angelica nodded, her smile still present but softened. "I'll make sure to close the door next time. Or perhaps move to softer pieces during class hours. That should help."

"That would be appreciated," John replied, glancing at the piano. "I understand you're enthusiastic about your program, but I'm trying to run a structured environment next door."

"Of course," she said, her voice as smooth as her playing. Then, tilting her head slightly, she added, "Though I've always found that a little music helps young minds focus. It inspires creativity."

John raised an eyebrow. "Creativity is all well and good, Miss Thompson, but I'm trying to teach grammar. I need their attention, not their inspiration."

Angelica's smile deepened, though there was a glint in her eye. "Duly noted. But I'd argue the two aren't mutually exclusive."

The silence stretched for a moment, the students watching the exchange like spectators at a tennis match.

John cleared his throat. "Well, I'll leave you to it, then. I trust you'll be mindful going forward."

"Absolutely, Mr. Anderson. I'll be sure to coordinate better next time."

"Thank you," he said, stepping back toward the door.

As he turned to leave, Angelica's voice stopped him. "You know, you're welcome to sit in on one of our sessions. You might enjoy it."

John hesitated but didn't look back. "Perhaps another time."

The door clicked shut behind him, and the faint sound of giggles resumed in the music room. Back in his classroom, the students were still humming softly, their pencils idle.

John picked up the chalk and tapped it against the board. "All right, class. Where were we?"

But as he spoke, a fragment of Angelica's music lingered in his mind, uninvited yet oddly pleasant.

Sing It Loud, Angelica!

The teacher's lounge was buzzing with the usual midday chatter—discussions about lesson plans, comparisons of misbehaving students, and the clinking of coffee mugs against saucers. John Anderson sat at the corner table, meticulously grading papers, his pencil moving with mechanical precision.

Across the room, Angelica Thompson breezed in, a sheet of paper clutched in her hand and a determined look on her face. Her cheeks were flushed from the cold, and wisps of her auburn hair had escaped her neatly pinned bun. She scanned the room, her eyes landing on Principal Harrison, who was pouring a fresh cup of coffee.

"Good afternoon, everyone," she said brightly, her voice cutting through the din. "I have an idea I'd like to share."

A few heads turned, including John's, though he didn't pause in his work.

Harrison smiled at her, always appreciative of Angelica's enthusiasm. "Miss Thompson, you've certainly piqued our interest. What's on your mind?"

Angelica unfolded the sheet of paper and held it up like a proclamation. "I propose that Jane's School hosts a community concert next month. A chance for the students to showcase their talents, bring parents together, and celebrate the holiday season."

The room fell quiet, save for the hiss of the radiator.

"A concert?" asked Mrs. Whitman, the first-grade teacher, lowering her knitting needles. "That's awfully ambitious, isn't it?"

"Ambitious but entirely possible," Angelica replied. "We already have a piano, and several students have shown great promise in our music sessions. They could perform solos or duets. Plus, we could have group singing numbers with every grade involved."

"That sounds like a lot of work," grumbled Mr. Cleary, the fifth-grade teacher, whose perpetual scowl made him look far older than his forty years. "Who's going to organize all this? We've got our hands full as it is."

Angelica's eyes sparkled. "I'd handle the logistics, of course. I'd work with the students, arrange the pieces, coordinate with parents for costumes, and plan the event schedule. All I'd need is your support in encouraging your students to participate."

Cleary snorted. "Support? Miss Thompson, you're asking us to add one more thing to our already packed schedules. And for what? A bit of singing and applause?"

"It's not just singing and applause," Angelica countered, her tone still sweet but tinged with steel. "Music builds confidence. It fosters collaboration and joy. Isn't that what we're all here for?"

"I think it's a lovely idea," Mrs. Whitman chimed in, though her voice wavered. "But what about funding? Wouldn't we need decorations? Programs? Refreshments?"

"Not necessarily," Angelica said. "We can keep it simple. The children could make decorations during art class—snowflakes, garlands, that sort of thing. Programs can be handwritten, and refreshments… Well, we can ask parents to contribute, potluck-style."

Principal Harrison stroked his chin thoughtfully. "Miss Thompson, I admire your enthusiasm, but you're asking for quite an undertaking. Do you really think you can pull it off in such a short time?"

"I do," Angelica said firmly. "The children are excited about music. They've been practicing diligently, and I've seen what they're capable of. This concert could be something special for them and their families. It's a chance to bring everyone together, especially with the holidays around the corner."

Harrison nodded slowly. "It's certainly an idea worth considering. But what do the rest of you think?"

All eyes turned to John, who had been uncharacteristically silent. He set down his pencil, carefully aligning it with the edge of the paper.

"It's… ambitious," he said finally. "And while I don't doubt Miss Thompson's dedication, I worry about the impact on the students' academic focus. This is their busiest time of year. Adding rehearsals might disrupt their studies."

Angelica turned to him, her expression soft but unwavering. "With respect, Mr. Anderson, academics aren't the only things that shape a child's education. Creativity, confidence, and joy are just as important. A concert like this can leave memories that last a lifetime."

John met her gaze, his brow furrowed. "Memories are all well and good, Miss Thompson, but not at the expense of their core education."

"It wouldn't be an expense," Angelica said. "It would be an enhancement. Imagine the shyest student in your class standing up and singing in front of an audience for the first time. That's a kind of growth that no textbook can teach."

The room went silent again, the tension evident.

Principal Harrison cleared his throat. "All right, then. Here's what we'll do. Miss Thompson, you have my permission to proceed. But keep it manageable—don't let it interfere with regular lessons. And you'll need to report back regularly on your progress."

Angelica's face broke into a radiant smile. "Thank you, Principal Harrison. I promise you won't regret it."

As she left the room, several teachers murmured among themselves. John returned to his grading, but a small part of him couldn't help wondering if Angelica might be right.

Back in the hall, Angelica passed the music room and placed her hand on the polished wood of the piano. "We'll show them," she whispered to herself. "They'll see."

Teamwork Makes the Concert Work

The sun was already dipping low in the sky, casting long shadows across the hallway as John Anderson locked his classroom door. The rhythmic tap of his footsteps echoed in the empty corridor as he passed the music room. The faint sound of a piano reached his ears, drawing his attention.

Through the glass-paneled door, he saw Angelica Thompson seated at the piano, her back straight, fingers moving across the keys in a slow, deliberate melody. Sheet music was scattered on the bench beside her, and her lips moved silently as she worked through a section of notes.

John hesitated. Since the staff meeting, her proposed concert had been a topic of quiet debate among the teachers. He had voiced his concerns but couldn't deny her resolve—and the surprising enthusiasm of the students. Clara Mayfield had mentioned just that afternoon how excited she was to be part of the group performance.

Before he fully realized what he was doing, John pushed open the door.

Angelica looked up, her fingers pausing mid-chord. A smile flickered across her face. "Mr. Anderson. To what do I owe the pleasure?"

"I didn't mean to interrupt," he said, stepping inside. "I was on my way out and… heard the music."

"Hard to resist, isn't it?" she teased lightly, turning back to the piano.

"I suppose so." He cleared his throat, clasping his hands behind his back. "I understand you've been busy preparing for the concert."

"Very busy," she said with a nod, gesturing to the scattered sheet music. "There's so much to organize—song arrangements, rehearsals, decorations, coordinating with parents… It's a lot to juggle, but I'm getting there."

John glanced at the chaos of papers and the overflowing stack of notes on the table beside her. He frowned slightly, then sighed. "Miss Thompson, if you'll forgive me, it seems you might have bitten off more than you can chew."

She looked at him, raising an eyebrow. "Is that an offer to help, Mr. Anderson? Or just an observation?"

John hesitated, caught off guard by her directness. "Well, I… I suppose it could be both."

Angelica's smile widened, and she shifted on the bench to face him fully. "Now this is a surprise. I thought you were against the concert."

"I was," he admitted. "I still have my reservations. But the students seem genuinely invested, and I… thought it might be worth lending a hand, if only to ensure it runs smoothly."

"I see." She studied him for a moment, then gestured to the seat beside her on the bench. "All right, Mr. Anderson. Let's see what you've got."

"I wasn't offering to play the piano," he said quickly, holding up his hands.

Angelica laughed. "Relax, I wouldn't dream of it. But if you're serious about helping, I could use another set of eyes on the logistics."

John eased onto the bench, stiff and unsure. He picked up a stack of papers, flipping through them with an almost academic focus. "What exactly do you need help with?"

"Well, for starters, scheduling. Rehearsals are getting tricky with so many kids involved. And there's the matter of the decorations—some of the other teachers are willing to have their students make them, but I need someone to help coordinate it all."

John nodded, scanning her haphazard notes. "These are… thorough, but they could use some organizing."

"Go ahead and say it—they're a mess," she said, grinning.

"I didn't say that."

"You didn't have to."

John set the papers down and leaned forward slightly, his brow furrowed in thought. "All right. I can help you create a proper schedule and coordinate with the other teachers for the decorations. I'll need a list of what you have in mind for each grade level."

Angelica looked at him, surprised. "You're really serious about this, aren't you?"

"If I commit to something, I do it properly," he replied.

"Noted." She leaned forward, her tone softening. "Thank you, Mr. Anderson. I know you've been skeptical about all this, but it means a lot to me—and the kids—that you're willing to help."

John met her gaze, something in her sincerity striking a chord he hadn't expected. "Just… let's keep it efficient. The less disruption to academics, the better."

"Of course," she said with a nod. "Though I have to warn you, Mr. Anderson—working with me might be a little less… orderly than you're used to."

"I'll manage," he said dryly, though a faint smile tugged at the corner of his mouth.

Angelica reached for a fresh sheet of paper and handed it to him, along with a pencil. "Then let's start with the schedule. Rehearsals are Mondays, Wednesdays, and Fridays after lunch. The older grades need more practice time, but I want everyone involved at least once a week…"

As they worked together, John found himself unexpectedly at ease. Angelica's energy was infectious, and her vision for the concert began to make sense in a way it hadn't before.

By the time they finished drafting a preliminary schedule, the sun had dipped below the horizon, and the music room was bathed in the soft glow of a single overhead light.

"Not bad for a first collaboration," Angelica said, holding up their work with satisfaction.

"Not bad," John agreed, though he wasn't entirely sure how it had happened. Somewhere between skepticism and practicality, he had become part of her plan.

A Standing Ovation for Miss Angelica

The gymnasium-turned-auditorium hummed with quiet anticipation. Rows of folding chairs were packed with parents, siblings, and a smattering of townsfolk who had come to see the school's first-ever concert. Paper snowflakes dangled from the ceiling, catching the glow of the stage lights, and garlands of construction paper draped the walls, lending the room a festive charm despite its humble decorations.

John stood near the back of the room, his arms folded, a skeptical expression masking his curiosity. He had spent the past few weeks assisting Angelica with the logistics—organizing the schedule, herding students to rehearsals, and even ensuring the piano was properly tuned. Yet, despite his involvement, he still harbored doubts. Was all this effort really worth the disruption it had caused?

The murmurs of the crowd fell silent as Angelica stepped onto the small stage. She wore a deep green dress that shimmered faintly under the lights, her auburn hair swept into an elegant twist. She smiled out at the audience, her hands clasped in front of her.

"Good evening, everyone," she began, her voice steady and warm. "Thank you all for being here tonight. This concert is more than just a performance—it's a celebration of our students, their hard work, and the joy they bring to our school every day."

A smattering of applause rippled through the crowd.

"For many of these children, this is their first time performing in front of an audience," Angelica continued. "It's not just about the music—it's about building confidence, creating memories, and sharing something beautiful with all of you. So, without further ado, let's begin!"

She stepped aside, and a group of first-graders shuffled onto the stage, clutching bells and tambourines. The music began with a simple rendition of *Jingle Bells*, the children grinning shyly as they shook their instruments in time with the melody.

The audience clapped enthusiastically, and John found himself smiling despite his reservations.

As the concert progressed, the performances grew more ambitious. A third-grade choir sang *Silent Night*, their young voices surprisingly harmonious. A fifth-grader played a solo on the violin, her bow trembling slightly at first but steadying as the song unfolded.

Then came the highlight of the evening—a piano duet by two sixth-graders, one of whom was Bobby Ferillo.

Bobby sat at the piano with the same confident air John had seen him adopt during rehearsals, his fingers poised over the keys. His partner, a quieter boy named Alan, took the upper register, their harmony precise and practiced. The piece was Beethoven's *Ode to Joy*, an ambitious choice that Angelica had guided them through with patience and determination.

The notes filled the gymnasium, resonating far beyond the humble setting. John's arms uncrossed as he leaned forward slightly, watching Bobby's hands glide over the keys with ease.

When the final chord echoed and faded, the audience erupted into applause. Bobby stood and bowed, his face alight with pride, while Alan beamed beside him.

Angelica returned to the stage, her smile radiant. "Let's hear it one more time for Bobby and Alan!"

As the clapping subsided, she addressed the audience. "And now, for our finale, I'd like to invite all our performers back to the stage for a special group number."

The stage filled with children of all ages, their faces a mixture of excitement and nerves. Angelica took her place at the piano and began to play the opening notes of *We Wish You a Merry Christmas*. The children joined in, their voices strong and full of life, as the audience clapped along.

John felt a lump rise in his throat. He hadn't expected this—a room filled with such warmth, such connection. For the first time, he understood what Angelica had been striving for. This wasn't just a concert. It was a moment that brought the school, the children, and the community together in a way that transcended academics.

When the final note sounded, the crowd rose to their feet in a standing ovation. Angelica bowed gracefully, then gestured to the children, encouraging them to take the applause they so richly deserved.

As the audience began to file out, John lingered near the door. Angelica approached him, her cheeks still flushed from the performance.

"Well, Mr. Anderson?" she said, tilting her head with a knowing smile. "What did you think?"

He hesitated, then nodded. "It was… remarkable. The children were remarkable. You were right—this was more than just music."

Angelica's smile deepened, and she reached out to lightly touch his arm. "I'm glad you think so. Thank you for helping make it happen. It wouldn't have been the same without you."

John looked down at her hand, then back into her eyes. "I'll admit, I wasn't sure about all of this at first. But seeing those kids up there tonight…" He paused, searching for the right words. "You've given them something special, Angelica. Something they'll remember."

"That's the idea," she said softly.

As the last of the crowd departed, leaving the gym quiet once more, John and Angelica stood together for a moment, sharing the stillness and the satisfaction of a job well done.

Secrets Over Coffee

The dim light of the music room's overhead fixture cast a warm glow over the polished black surface of the piano. It was late, and the usual hum of the school had settled into silence, save for the faint rustle of papers as Angelica tidied up after the day's rehearsals.

John lingered in the doorway, one hand resting lightly on the frame. He hadn't intended to stop by—he'd been heading out to his car after finishing his grading—but the soft strains of Angelica's humming had drawn him like a moth to a flame.

"You're still here," he said, his voice quiet but enough to break the stillness.

Angelica glanced up, startled, then smiled. "And so are you, Mr. Anderson. Late night?"

"You could say that," he replied, stepping into the room. He gestured to the sheet music scattered across the piano bench. "Preparing for the next big concert already?"

Angelica laughed lightly, stacking the papers into a neat pile. "Not yet. Just wrapping up for the day. Rehearsals went longer than expected, as usual."

John nodded, his gaze drifting to the piano. "The students seem to love it, though. They're more enthusiastic than I ever imagined."

"That's the magic of music," she said, sliding onto the bench. Her fingers idly grazed the keys, playing a few quiet notes. "It's always been that way for me, at least. My greatest teacher, my most constant companion."

John moved closer, leaning against the piano's edge. "How did it start for you?"

Angelica paused, her eyes softening as she stared down at the keys. "It started with my father. He was a church organist, and every Sunday after services, he'd let me climb up onto the bench with him. I couldn't even reach the pedals, but he'd guide my hands over the keys and let me play little melodies."

She smiled faintly, the memory lighting her features. "I must've been six or seven. He used to say, 'Angelica, music is the voice of the soul. When words fail, let the music speak.'"

John tilted his head, intrigued. "Wise man."

"He was," she said softly. "He passed away when I was fourteen, but his lessons stayed with me. My mother, too—she was a piano teacher. I think they always knew music would be my path."

John watched her hands as they hovered over the keys, her fingers tracing invisible notes. "So you always knew you'd teach?"

"Not always," Angelica admitted, looking up at him. "I thought for a time I'd be a concert pianist. I even got a scholarship to study at a conservatory. But…"

"But?"

She shrugged, a bittersweet smile tugging at her lips. "I realized performing wasn't what I wanted. Don't get me wrong—I love playing. But standing on a stage, playing for strangers? It felt… hollow. What I really wanted was to share the joy of music, to help others find their voice through it. Teaching felt more fulfilling. So I changed course."

"That's quite a decision," John said.

"Maybe," she said. "But it was the right one for me. There's something extraordinary about seeing a child light up when they finally master a piece or sing in front of an audience for the first time. It's magic, pure and simple."

John crossed his arms, his gaze thoughtful. "It's not so different from what I've always believed about teaching. Helping a student unlock their potential, watching them grow into themselves—it's why I'm here, too."

Angelica smiled at him, her expression warm. "See? We're not so different after all, Mr. Anderson."

He chuckled softly. "I suppose not."

She shifted on the bench, patting the space beside her. "Why don't you sit? You've been standing there like a sentinel long enough."

He hesitated, then sat down, keeping a polite distance.

"Do you play?" Angelica asked, her eyes twinkling.

"Not since I was a boy," John admitted. "My mother taught me a few basic pieces on our old upright piano, but I was more interested in reading than practicing."

"Fair enough," she said, her fingers returning to the keys. She began to play a simple, soothing tune, the notes soft and inviting.

For a moment, neither of them spoke, the music filling the space between them. John found himself relaxing, the tension he so often carried easing in the quiet of the moment.

"What about you?" Angelica asked suddenly, her voice low. "Why did you decide to teach?"

John considered her question, his gaze fixed on the piano. "My father was a teacher. A good one. He believed education was the key to everything—opportunity, understanding, growth. I suppose I wanted to follow in his footsteps, though I never imagined I'd end up here."

"You've done well, though," Angelica said, her tone sincere. "This school, these children—they're lucky to have you."

He glanced at her, a flicker of surprise crossing his face. "Thank you. That means more than you know."

Angelica's hands stilled on the keys, and she turned to face him fully. "And I'm lucky to have found this place. To have found… this team. You've been more supportive than I expected, John. Even when you didn't agree with me."

John met her gaze, his expression softening. "It's easy to support someone who cares as much as you do, Angelica."

The room fell silent again, the weight of the moment settling between them. Outside, the wind rustled the bare branches of the great maples, the sound faint but grounding.

Angelica smiled, then returned to the piano. "Well, Mr. Anderson, if you're lucky, one day I might teach you to play properly."

"Don't hold your breath," John replied, though there was a rare warmth in his voice.

For the first time, John felt that their paths as colleagues—and perhaps friends—had truly aligned.

Leaves and Lessons

The late afternoon sun cast golden light across the schoolyard, illuminating the two great maples that stood sentinel on either side of the entrance. Their broad canopies, newly adorned with fresh green leaves, seemed to shimmer in the gentle breeze.

John paused at the window of his classroom, gazing out at the scene as his students quietly worked on their assignments. The rhythmic scratch of pencils on paper and the occasional shuffle of chairs faded into the background as he focused on the trees.

The maples had always been there, or so he imagined. Strong and steadfast, their roots dug deep into the earth, they seemed eternal—an anchor for the school and the generations of children who had passed through its doors. Now, as their leaves danced and quivered in the spring breeze, they reminded him of something else: renewal.

"Mr. Anderson?"

The voice pulled him from his reverie. He turned to see Clara Mayfield standing beside his desk, holding her worksheet in both hands.

"I'm finished," she said softly, her round face peering up at him with a mixture of pride and uncertainty.

"Let's have a look," John said, taking the paper and scanning it. The sentence diagram was neat, her lines straight and precise.

"Very good, Clara," he said, handing it back to her. "Keep up the good work."

Her smile brightened as she returned to her seat, and John's gaze shifted once again to the window. Beyond the maples, the playground was scattered with children's toys—an abandoned ball, a jump rope tangled in the grass.

Angelica's voice echoed faintly from the music room down the hall, accompanied by the soft strains of the piano. The two sounds wove together, creating a quiet harmony that seemed to fill the school with life.

John stepped closer to the window, placing his hands on the cool glass. He watched as a particularly strong gust sent the young leaves fluttering wildly before settling them again.

For a moment, he imagined the leaves as symbols of growth—each one a snapshot of new beginnings, fresh starts, and boundless potential. How many children had played beneath these trees over the decades? How many of those children now had children of their own?

He thought about his own place in the school's history. He was new here, yes, but the school already felt like an extension of himself. He wondered if, years from now, someone else would stand in this very spot, watching the leaves sway and reflecting on their own journey.

The thought was both comforting and exhilarating.

"Spring is beautiful, isn't it?"

The voice startled him, and he turned to see Angelica standing in the doorway. She held a stack of sheet music, her auburn hair catching the golden light from the window.

"It is," John replied, glancing back outside.

She stepped into the room, setting the music on the corner of his desk. "I've always loved autumn—the colors, the crisp air. But there's something about spring. It's raw and alive, full of promise. You can't help but feel hopeful."

John nodded, still watching the trees. "It reminds me how everything starts fresh. These leaves, the seasons... even us, in a way."

Angelica followed his gaze, her expression softening. "That's true. And it's part of what makes spring so special. It's not just about what's growing—it's about what's enduring. The trees were here before us, and they'll be here long after. They remind us to keep going."

He glanced at her, studying the quiet conviction in her face. "I suppose you're right."

They stood in silence for a moment, the sounds of the school fading into the background as they both watched the leaves.

"I saw your students practicing for the concert this morning," John said, breaking the quiet. "They seemed... eager."

"They are," Angelica said, her smile returning. "Some of them were nervous at first, but they're finding their confidence. It's amazing how quickly they come alive when they're given a chance to shine."

John nodded. "You've brought something special to this place, Angelica. The children feel it, and so does the staff."

Her cheeks flushed slightly, and she looked down at her hands. "Thank you, John. That means a lot, coming from you."

The silence returned, but this time it felt companionable.

John finally turned away from the window, the weight of his thoughts settling into something quieter, more manageable. "I should get back to grading."

"And I need to sort this music," Angelica said, picking up the stack from his desk.

As she turned to leave, she paused at the door. "You know, John, you're like those trees out there. Steady, dependable. But don't forget that even the strongest trees need time to grow, to change."

Her words lingered as she left the room, her footsteps fading down the hall.

John looked out at the maples one last time, watching their leaves tremble in the breeze. He didn't have all the answers, but for the first time in a long while, he felt a small flicker of anticipation.

Change wasn't something to fear, he thought. Perhaps it was something to nurture.

A Question of Courage

1958

The late afternoon sun slanted through the tall windows of the music room, bathing it in a warm glow. Angelica Thompson stood at the piano, sorting through sheet music and humming a soft melody to herself. She paused now and then to gaze out at the budding trees that framed the schoolyard.

There was a faint creak at the door, and Angelica glanced up, her heart leaping at the sight of John Anderson standing hesitantly in the doorway. He looked serious—too serious—and she immediately felt a flicker of hope. *Is this it?* she thought. *Is he finally going to ask me?*

"John," she greeted him warmly, setting the sheet music down. "What brings you by?"

John stepped inside, his hat clutched tightly in one hand. "Angelica," he began, his tone formal. "I, uh… I wanted to talk to you about something."

She smiled, her green eyes sparkling with curiosity. "Well, you've found me. What's on your mind?"

He hesitated, shifting his weight from one foot to the other, his usual composure nowhere to be found. "You've probably noticed," he started awkwardly, "that I've been… around. More than usual, I mean."

Angelica tilted her head slightly, suppressing a smile. "I've noticed."

John looked down, a faint flush creeping into his cheeks. "It's just… I enjoy your company. You're easy to talk to, and… well, you're not just a good teacher. You're remarkable, Angelica. And I—"

Her heart raced as she waited, her hands clasped behind her back to keep from betraying her excitement.

John took a deep breath, then released it in a rush of words. "Would you like to have dinner with me this weekend?"

For a moment, Angelica simply stared at him, her breath caught in her chest. She'd imagined this moment a hundred times, and now that it was here, it felt both surreal and perfect.

"I'd love to," she said, her voice soft but clear.

John's face broke into a relieved smile, his shoulders relaxing. "You would?"

"Of course, I would," Angelica replied, stepping closer to him. "I've been waiting for you to ask."

He blinked, startled. "You have?"

She laughed, a musical sound that seemed to fill the room. "John Anderson, you're not as subtle as you think. But I'm glad you worked up the courage."

He chuckled, running a hand through his hair. "Well, I didn't want to assume. You deserve someone who—"

"Stop," she interrupted gently, placing a hand on his arm. "You don't have to justify this. I like you, John. I have for a while."

John's smile widened, his confidence returning. "Well, then. It's settled. Dinner it is."

"It's a date," Angelica said with a grin.

They stood in comfortable silence for a moment, the hum of the piano and the chirping of birds outside the only sounds.

"I should get going," John said reluctantly. "Still have papers to grade."

"And I need to finish sorting this music," Angelica replied, though she made no move to return to her task.

He lingered at the door, his hand on the frame. "Thank you, Angelica."

"For what?"

"For being patient with me."

Her smile softened. "Some things are worth waiting for."

As he stepped out into the hallway, Angelica turned back to the piano, her heart light and her thoughts full of possibilities. She played a quiet melody, her fingers gliding effortlessly over the keys.

And for the first time, she allowed herself to imagine what the future might hold—a future that felt just a little brighter, now that John had taken the first step.

A Night to Remember

Saturday arrived with the kind of spring weather that seemed plucked from a storybook. The air was warm but fresh, and the sun hung low in the sky, casting golden light over the town. Angelica stood in front of her small vanity, smoothing the skirt of her favorite green dress. Her hands trembled slightly—not from nerves, but from excitement.

John Anderson had always been a man of quiet consistency, but something told her tonight would reveal sides of him she hadn't yet seen.

At exactly six o'clock, there was a knock at her door. Angelica's heart fluttered as she opened it to find John standing there, looking as polished and nervous as she'd ever seen him. He wore a neatly pressed suit and tie, his hair combed with an extra layer of care. In his hands, he held a single daffodil.

"For you," he said, his voice warm but tentative.

Angelica's smile was bright enough to rival the setting sun. "It's beautiful. Thank you, John."

He cleared his throat, glancing toward the street. "Shall we?"

She took his offered arm, her curiosity mounting as he led her to a sleek, borrowed car—a shiny black beauty that looked as though it had rolled off a movie set.

"This isn't your car," she said, arching an eyebrow.

John chuckled, holding the door open for her. "No, it's not. Mr. Cleary offered it to me for the evening. Said it would add some... flair."

Angelica laughed softly as she slid into the seat, the faint scent of leather and polished wood surrounding her. "It certainly does."

John climbed into the driver's seat, glancing at her with a small, self-deprecating smile. "I figured our first date deserved something special."

"It already is," she said sincerely.

He drove them out of town, the road winding through the hills as the golden light faded into dusk. Angelica watched the scenery pass by, the growing sense of wonder in her chest matched by the quiet determination on John's face.

They arrived at a small, tucked-away restaurant she'd never seen before, its stone facade glowing with the warm light of lanterns. A hand-painted sign above the door read *Le Jardin*, its delicate script as inviting as the faint strains of violin music drifting from within.

"Le Jardin?" Angelica repeated, raising an eyebrow.

"I asked around," John admitted, offering her his arm again as they approached the door. "Mrs. Whitman said this was the nicest spot within fifty miles. Thought you'd like it."

As they stepped inside, Angelica was struck by the charm of the place. It was intimate, with just a handful of tables draped in white linens, vases of fresh flowers as centerpieces. The soft glow of candlelight and the gentle music created a magical atmosphere.

A waiter appeared, greeting them with a warm smile and leading them to a corner table near a window that overlooked a small garden.

"This is incredible," Angelica said, her voice tinged with awe as they sat.

John looked both pleased and relieved. "I wasn't sure if it'd be your style."

"It's perfect," she said, reaching across the table to touch his hand briefly.

The dinner was nothing short of enchanting. John surprised her with his humor, sharing stories of his childhood with a dry wit that had her laughing until her cheeks ached. Angelica, in turn, shared tales of her own—a mischievous escapade at her piano recital as a child, the time she accidentally orchestrated a schoolwide singalong by starting a song in the hallways.

"You've always been a leader," John said with a smile, his gaze steady and admiring.

"And you've always been dependable," she replied, her voice softer now. "I see it every day at school—how much the children and staff respect you."

John glanced down, his ears turning faintly pink. "I just try to do what's right."

"You do," Angelica said, her green eyes bright. "And that's what makes you extraordinary."

John's throat bobbed as he swallowed, clearly unused to such praise. But there was a flicker of pride in his expression—a quiet acceptance of her words.

After dinner, he surprised her again by suggesting a walk through the garden behind the restaurant. The night air was cool, the stars sparkling like diamonds in the inky sky.

They strolled along the winding paths, pausing occasionally to admire the flowers bathed in moonlight.

"I don't know how you planned all this," Angelica said, her voice full of wonder. "But it's the most thoughtful thing anyone's ever done for me."

John stopped beside a stone bench, turning to face her. "You're worth it, Angelica."

Her breath caught at the sincerity in his voice, her heart swelling with a warmth she hadn't expected.

He glanced down, his hands in his pockets. "I wasn't sure I'd ever find someone like you—someone who understands how much this school means to me, how much I want to build a life that matters. But then you came along, and… I don't know. It feels like you were meant to be here."

Angelica smiled, stepping closer. "I've always believed that people come into our lives for a reason. And I think you might be right, John."

They stood there in the quiet garden, the world around them fading into the background. For the first time, John reached for her hand, his touch tentative but firm.

"I'm not great with words," he said, his voice low. "But I hope tonight showed you how I feel."

"It did," Angelica replied, her voice steady but brimming with emotion.

They lingered there for a moment longer, the stars above them and the faint scent of flowers in the air.

It was a first date neither of them would ever forget—a night that marked the beginning of a partnership as steady and enduring as the roots of the great maples back at Jane's School.

A Ring, a Piano, and a Question

1959

The faint glow of the setting sun streamed through the tall windows of the music room, casting golden patches on the polished floor. The piano stood in its usual place, timeless and elegant, its black surface gleaming in the soft light.

John Anderson adjusted his tie for the third time, his palms uncharacteristically clammy. He stood just outside the door, gripping a small velvet box in his hand, his heart pounding harder than it had since his first day at Jane's School.

From inside the room came the familiar sound of Angelica playing. Her fingers danced lightly over the keys, coaxing a soft, wistful melody that filled the air. The music seemed to wrap around John, both calming and intensifying his nerves.

He took a deep breath, straightened his shoulders, and stepped inside.

Angelica looked up from the piano, her expression brightening as she saw him. "John! I wasn't expecting you. What brings you here so late?"

"I—uh—was finishing some work," he said, his voice steadier than he felt. "I saw the light on and thought I'd stop by."

She smiled, her auburn hair catching the warm glow from the windows. "You're always welcome here, you know that."

He nodded, moving closer to the piano. The velvet box felt impossibly heavy in his pocket.

Angelica shifted slightly on the bench, patting the space beside her. "Come, sit. I was just experimenting with something new."

John hesitated, then eased onto the bench, careful to leave a polite distance between them.

"What are you working on?" he asked, though his thoughts were elsewhere.

"Just a little melody I've been playing with," she said, her fingers gliding over the keys. "I haven't decided where it's going yet, but it feels… hopeful."

The music swirled around them, soft and inviting, as Angelica's focus returned to the piano. John watched her, the way her hands moved with grace and precision, the way her face lit up when she played. He had always admired her passion, her ability to create something beautiful out of nothing.

"Angelica," he said suddenly, the word coming out more forcefully than he intended.

She stopped playing and turned to him, her green eyes filled with curiosity. "Yes?"

John reached into his pocket, his fingers brushing against the box. "There's something I've been meaning to say. Something I've wanted to say for a while now."

Angelica tilted her head, a small smile playing on her lips. "Go on, then."

He swallowed hard, his heart hammering in his chest. "I never expected to find someone like you. Someone who... challenges me, inspires me. You've changed the way I see the world, the way I see myself. And every day, I look forward to seeing you, to working with you, to... just being near you."

Angelica's smile softened, her eyes searching his face.

John took the box from his pocket and opened it, revealing a simple gold ring with a small, elegant diamond. "Angelica Thompson, will you marry me?"

For a moment, the room was silent, the music from the piano lingering like a memory in the air.

Angelica's eyes glistened as she reached out, her hand trembling slightly as she touched the ring. "Oh, John..."

She looked up at him, her expression filled with warmth and joy. "Yes. Yes, I will."

John exhaled, the tension leaving his body in a rush. He took her hand, slipping the ring onto her finger with care. It fit perfectly.

Angelica laughed softly, a sound like music itself, and threw her arms around him. John hesitated for only a moment before wrapping his arms around her, holding her close.

When they finally pulled back, Angelica's hands remained on his shoulders, her eyes shining. "You're full of surprises, John Anderson."

"I figured it was about time," he said, his usual composure returning with a faint smile. "Though I did worry you might think it was too soon."

"Too soon?" Angelica shook her head, her auburn hair catching the fading light. "John, I've known for months. I've been waiting for you to catch up."

They both laughed, the sound filling the room, echoing off the walls like a duet.

Angelica turned back to the piano, her fingers drifting over the keys. "I think this calls for some music, don't you?"

"What did you have in mind?"

She played a soft, romantic tune, glancing at him with a twinkle in her eye. "Something hopeful, of course."

John leaned slightly closer, letting the music envelop them both. For the first time in his life, he wasn't thinking about tomorrow's lesson plan or the endless responsibilities of his job.

For the first time, he was simply present, savoring the moment and the promise of what was to come.

Happily Ever After, School Edition

1960

The chapel was small but filled with warmth, its simple wooden pews adorned with white ribbons and sprigs of evergreen. Sunlight streamed through the stained-glass windows, casting colorful patches on the stone floor. The scent of fresh flowers mingled with the faint hint of wax from the candles flickering on the altar.

John stood at the front of the aisle, his hands clasped tightly in front of him. Dressed in a sharp black suit with a white rose pinned to his lapel, he felt an unfamiliar mix of nerves and joy coursing through him. The room was filled with familiar faces—colleagues, students, townsfolk—all there to witness this day. Yet, for all the eyes on him, his attention was focused solely on the woman stepping into view.

Angelica entered the chapel on her brother's arm, her gown simple yet elegant, the lace train whispering across the floor as she walked. Her auburn hair was swept into soft curls, a crown of white blossoms nestled among them. She radiated a quiet confidence that John had always admired, her green eyes meeting his as she approached.

The music from the small string quartet swelled, filling the room with a melody that seemed to echo the beating of John's heart. Angelica's smile was soft, but her gaze was steady, reassuring him as she reached the altar.

"You look beautiful," John whispered as her brother stepped back, leaving them face to face.

"And you look nervous," Angelica replied with a playful twinkle in her eye.

The officiant cleared his throat, and the ceremony began. The words of the vows seemed to blur together in John's mind, though he repeated them with unwavering certainty. When it was Angelica's turn, her voice was clear and strong, each word imbued with meaning.

When the rings were exchanged, John slid the band onto Angelica's finger, his hands steadier than he'd expected. As she did the same for him, her fingers brushed his, sending a small thrill through him.

"By the power vested in me," the officiant declared, "I now pronounce you husband and wife. You may kiss the bride."

John leaned in, their first kiss as husband and wife as natural as breathing. The room erupted into applause, the sound filling the chapel and spilling out into the crisp winter air.

The reception was held in the school's gymnasium, decorated for the occasion with strings of white lights and bouquets of winter blooms. The piano, polished to a shine, sat in the corner, a small ensemble playing lively tunes as guests mingled.

John stood near the refreshment table, holding a cup of coffee and watching Angelica as she moved through the room, her laugh ringing out as she greeted well-wishers.

"She's quite something," Principal Harrison said, stepping up beside him.

"She is," John replied, his voice soft.

"You're lucky, Anderson. But then again, so is she. You make a good team."

John nodded, glancing down at the simple gold band now resting on his finger. "We do."

As the evening wound down, the guests slowly began to leave, their well-wishes lingering in the air. John and Angelica found themselves alone in the music room, the flickering candlelight casting shadows on the walls.

Angelica sat at the piano, her fingers playing a slow, tender melody. John leaned against the doorframe, watching her with a quiet smile.

"Do you think we can do it?" he asked after a moment.

She looked up, her hands stilling on the keys. "Do what?"

"Build the life we've talked about. Dedicate ourselves to the school, to the children. To each other."

Angelica's expression softened, and she stood, crossing the room to him. She took his hands in hers, their fingers interlacing. "Of course we can, John. Together, we can do anything."

He nodded, his doubts easing in the light of her conviction. "Then I promise you this: I'll give everything I have to make that happen. To support you, the school, and our students."

"And I promise," Angelica said, her voice steady, "to stand beside you, no matter what challenges come our way. This school—it's part of us now. And I can't imagine a better partner to share it with."

They held each other for a long moment, the music room silent save for the faint rustle of leaves outside the window.

It wasn't just a wedding day. It was the beginning of a life built on shared purpose, love, and the belief that together, they could make a difference.

Little Bobby, Big Dreams

1961

The faint notes of a piano echoed through the halls of Jane's School as Angelica Thompson prepared for her afternoon music class. The soft sound wasn't hers; she hadn't begun the day's lesson yet. Intrigued, she stepped into the music room and paused, listening.

The notes weren't perfect—some stumbled transitions, uneven pacing—but there was an undeniable spark behind the playing. Someone was experimenting, exploring, their touch tentative but full of potential.

Angelica moved toward the source, her eyes falling on a boy seated at the piano. He was small for his age, his dark hair slightly messy and his posture rigid as he peered intently at the keys. His fingers moved carefully, playing the opening bars of *Für Elise*.

"Bobby Ferillo," Angelica said gently, stepping closer.

The boy flinched, his hands freezing mid-note. He turned, wide-eyed. "I—I'm sorry, Miss Thompson. I wasn't supposed to—"

"No need to apologize," Angelica said, her voice warm as she took a seat on the bench beside him. "That was quite good, actually. Do you play often?"

Bobby shook his head quickly. "No, ma'am. I just... I hear things sometimes, and I try to copy them. I didn't mean to touch the piano. It's just... It sounded so nice, and I wanted to try."

Angelica smiled, sensing his nervousness. "Well, I'm glad you did. You've got a good ear, Bobby. You knew where the notes should go, even if you weren't sure how to make them perfect."

Bobby's cheeks flushed. "It's not as good as when you play. It's probably dumb."

"It's not dumb," Angelica said firmly. "It's a gift. Do you know how many people would give anything to be able to sit down and play like you just did, without any lessons?"

Bobby shrugged, but there was a flicker of pride in his eyes. "I just like how it sounds."

Angelica placed her hands on the keys, playing a soft melody. "Music isn't about being perfect, Bobby. It's about expression. It's about how it makes you feel and how it connects you to others. Do you know what I mean?"

Bobby nodded slowly. "I think so."

Angelica stopped playing and turned to him. "Would you like to learn? I could teach you, if you're willing to put in the effort."

His face lit up, but then hesitation clouded his features. "I don't know if my parents could pay for lessons."

Angelica shook her head. "You don't have to worry about that. We can practice during lunch breaks or after school, here in the music room. If you want to, that is."

Bobby's grin was answer enough. "I'd like that. I'd like that a lot."

The weeks that followed became a routine. Every day after lunch, Bobby would slip into the music room, where Angelica would have a new piece of music waiting for him. At first, they worked on basic exercises—scales, simple melodies—but it wasn't long before Bobby's natural talent began to shine.

One afternoon, as Angelica showed him a new technique, Principal Harrison appeared in the doorway. He leaned against the frame, watching as Bobby played a section of *Clair de Lune*, his hands moving across the keys with growing confidence.

"He's something, isn't he?" Harrison said softly when the piece ended.

Angelica turned to him, her smile proud. "He has an incredible ear. He picks things up faster than some adults I've taught."

Bobby flushed at the praise, looking down at his hands. "I just like learning from Miss Thompson."

"Well, I'd say you've got the right teacher," Harrison said, nodding approvingly.

One day, after their practice session, Angelica asked Bobby, "Do you ever think about what you'd like to do when you're older?"

Bobby thought for a moment, his fingers idly pressing random keys. "I think... maybe I'd like to keep playing. Maybe I could even teach someday, like you."

Angelica's heart swelled at the words. She reached out, placing a hand on his shoulder. "You can do anything you want, Bobby. You have the talent, but more importantly, you have the passion. Never lose that."

From that day on, Bobby's confidence grew, and so did his dreams. Angelica knew she had found something extraordinary in him—not just a gifted musician, but a child who had found his voice through music.

And as she watched him play, his fingers now sure and steady, she realized how much he had taught her, too. Music wasn't just about the notes. It was about giving someone the chance to believe in themselves, to discover who they were meant to be.

Tom's Test Blues

1962

The classroom was quiet except for the occasional rustle of papers and the soft tick of the clock on the wall. John Anderson sat at his desk, his attention focused on the stack of graded quizzes before him. He picked up another sheet, its edges slightly crumpled, and scanned the answers.

Tom Ferillo's name was written at the top, his uneven handwriting making the letters tilt awkwardly to the right. John's brow furrowed as he reached the end of the page. The red pen in his hand moved carefully, marking corrections and circling incomplete answers.

The grade was not a good one.

Moments later, the bell rang, signaling the end of the school day. Students filed out in pairs and clusters, their voices rising in animated chatter. John noticed Tom lingering near the door, his head down, his books held tightly to his chest.

"Tom," John called, his voice calm but firm.

The boy stopped and turned slowly, his face a mask of apprehension. "Yes, Mr. Anderson?"

"Come here for a moment," John said, gesturing to the desk.

Tom shuffled forward, his shoulders hunched as if bracing for bad news.

John held up the quiz. "I wanted to talk to you about this."

Tom's face turned red, and he stared at the floor. "I know. I didn't do good."

John softened his tone. "No, you didn't do as well as I know you're capable of. But I'd like to understand why. What happened?"

Tom hesitated, fidgeting with the edge of his book. "I don't know. I studied, I swear. It's just… it doesn't stick. And then I get in here, and my brain gets all jumbled."

John nodded, listening carefully. "That happens sometimes. Especially when you're trying too hard to get everything perfect."

Tom's eyes darted up briefly. "I didn't want you to be mad."

"I'm not mad, Tom," John said firmly. "I'm here to help you, but I can't do that if you don't tell me what's going on. Is it the material? Something outside of school?"

Tom's lips pressed into a thin line before he muttered, "It's Bobby."

John raised an eyebrow. "Your brother?"

Tom nodded, his voice barely above a whisper. "He's good at everything. Music, school, everything. I'm not. I'm just… me."

John set the quiz down and leaned forward, resting his elbows on the desk. "Tom, let me tell you something. Being you is more than enough. You don't have to be Bobby. You don't have to be anyone but yourself."

"But I'm not good at anything," Tom said, his voice cracking.

"That's not true," John said. "You're good at a lot of things. I see it every day. You're curious, you're kind, and you don't give up, even when things are hard. Those are qualities that matter far more than any grade on a quiz."

Tom's brow furrowed. "But grades are important, aren't they?"

"They are," John agreed. "But they're not the only thing that defines you. And if you're struggling, it doesn't mean you're failing—it means we need to find a better way to help you understand."

Tom looked at him, a flicker of hope in his eyes. "You really think so?"

"I know so," John said. He tapped the quiz lightly. "Why don't we start with this? Come in during lunch tomorrow, and we'll go over the material together. We'll figure out where you're getting stuck and take it one step at a time."

Tom hesitated, then nodded. "Okay."

"Good," John said with a small smile. "And Tom?"

"Yes, sir?"

"Don't be so hard on yourself. Everyone learns differently. The important thing is that you keep trying."

Tom gave a shy smile, the tension in his shoulders easing slightly. "Thanks, Mr. Anderson."

"Anytime," John said.

As Tom left the room, his steps a little lighter, John leaned back in his chair. He glanced at the quiz again and made a mental note to look for additional ways to support Tom.

Helping students like Tom wasn't about test scores or grades. It was about seeing the person behind the struggle and giving them the tools—and the confidence—to find their way.

Progress? Not on My Watch!

1963

The teachers' lounge buzzed with the usual hum of midday chatter as staff gathered for their lunch break. John Anderson sat at the corner table, absently stirring sugar into his coffee. Around him, conversations about lesson plans and upcoming school events mingled with the clatter of coffee cups and the scrape of chairs against the tiled floor.

Principal Harrison entered with a clipboard tucked under his arm, his demeanor unusually brisk. The conversations quieted as he reached the center of the room.

"Ladies and gentlemen," Harrison began, his tone suggesting he was about to deliver something significant. "I've been speaking with the school board, and we're moving forward with installing a new intercom system throughout the building."

The room erupted into a mix of murmurs and exclamations.

"An intercom system?" Mrs. Whitman, the first-grade teacher, said, her voice tinged with surprise. "Is that really necessary?"

"It will allow us to communicate more efficiently," Harrison explained, setting the clipboard on the counter. "Announcements, alerts, reminders—everything will be centralized. It's part of the board's modernization initiative."

"That's one word for it," Mr. Cleary muttered from his spot by the coffee pot. "Sounds like a lot of noise to me."

"I think it's a wonderful idea," Angelica said, her expression thoughtful. "It could be useful during emergencies, and it might even save time during the day."

Several heads nodded in agreement, but others remained skeptical.

John leaned back in his chair, his brow furrowed. "I'm not so sure this is the right move."

All eyes turned to him, the quiet authority in his voice commanding attention.

"And why's that, Mr. Anderson?" Harrison asked, raising an eyebrow.

"Because this school runs just fine as it is," John replied. "We've been using written notices and face-to-face communication for years. It works. An intercom might save a few minutes here and there, but at what cost? It's an unnecessary disruption."

"Disruption?" Angelica asked, tilting her head. "I don't see how it would disrupt anything. If anything, it could make things more streamlined."

"Streamlined, perhaps," John conceded, "but also impersonal. What's wrong with walking to a classroom and speaking to a teacher directly? Or sending a student with a note? Those interactions mean something. An intercom reduces everything to a faceless announcement."

Cleary grunted in agreement. "And imagine the racket during the day. Ding-dong, this, ding-dong, that. We'll have kids thinking they're at the train station."

A few chuckles rippled through the room, but Angelica remained thoughtful. "I understand your concerns, John, but we have to think about the bigger picture. Progress isn't always comfortable, but that doesn't mean it isn't necessary. Schools everywhere are modernizing. Shouldn't we keep up?"

John's jaw tightened. "Keeping up for the sake of it isn't reason enough. Change needs to serve a purpose, not just follow a trend."

"But isn't the purpose clear?" Angelica countered, her tone calm but firm. "Efficiency, safety, and keeping our school connected. Progress isn't about replacing traditions—it's about adapting them to make things better."

The room fell silent, the tension between practicality and tradition hanging thick in the air.

Harrison cleared his throat. "Let's not forget that this decision isn't entirely ours. The school board has already approved the funding, and the installation is scheduled to begin next month. I called this meeting to inform you, not to open the matter for debate."

John's lips pressed into a thin line. He understood the principal's position, but the announcement still left him unsettled.

"Progress is fine," John said finally, his voice measured, "but it should never come at the expense of what makes this school special. Let's just hope this intercom doesn't turn into a symbol of what we're losing."

The room remained quiet for a moment before the conversations resumed in smaller, quieter groups.

Angelica approached John as he stood to leave. "You know," she said softly, "progress doesn't have to be the enemy of tradition. Sometimes it can help preserve what's important."

John glanced at her, his expression unreadable. "Maybe. But it's the 'sometimes' that worries me."

Angelica gave him a small, understanding smile. "You'll see, John. Change isn't always bad."

John nodded faintly but didn't reply. As he left the lounge, the faint buzz of conversation followed him, though his mind remained preoccupied with thoughts of what the intercom—and what it represented—might mean for the school he had come to cherish.

The sound of footsteps quickened behind him, light but purposeful.

"John, wait!"

He slowed, turning to see Angelica coming toward him, her auburn hair catching the light filtering through the windows. She wore the faintly apologetic smile he knew so well, her sheet music still tucked under one arm.

"Are you upset with me?" she asked, her tone quiet but direct.

John blinked, surprised. "Upset? Angelica, why would I be upset?"

"Well," she said, stepping closer, "I spoke against you in front of everyone. I know how much this school means to you, and I know how you feel about... all this modernization."

He tilted his head, studying her. "So, you think I'd be upset because you spoke your mind?"

Her eyes searched his, unsure. "You seemed... tense."

John sighed, softening. He reached out, resting a hand gently on her arm. "Angelica, I want you to speak your mind. Always. Especially when you disagree with me."

"You mean that?"

He smiled faintly. "Of course, I mean it. You challenge me, Angelica. You make me think, and that's something I'll never take for granted. I might not always agree, but I'll always value what you have to say. You know that."

Her shoulders relaxed, the tension leaving her posture. "I do. I just—"

"Just what?" he prompted gently.

"I don't want you to feel like I don't support you," she admitted, her voice quieter now.

John's hand slid down to take hers, his fingers warm against hers. "You support me in every way that matters. And you know, it's because of you that I'm willing to rethink things, even if I don't say it out loud right away."

Her lips curved into a soft smile. "That's good to hear, because I'll admit I'm rethinking some things, too."

"Like what?"

"Like whether this intercom really is the perfect solution," she said with a playful glint in her eye. "Cleary had a point—it might feel a little like a train station with all the ding-dongs."

John chuckled, shaking his head. "I suppose I should thank him for that colorful image."

Angelica squeezed his hand. "Progress doesn't have to come at the expense of what's special here. You're right about that, John. But sometimes, it can help protect what we love. That's all I was trying to say."

John nodded, his smile lingering. "And I hear you. I might even see your point—eventually."

She laughed softly, her voice light and musical, the tension between them dissolving.

They began walking down the hall together, the warmth of their shared understanding enveloping them.

"You know," John said, glancing at her, "I always thought you preferred autumn over spring."

"I do," she replied, her tone thoughtful. "Autumn has this quiet beauty—everything slowing down, preparing for rest. It's comforting."

He tilted his head. "Spring's always been my favorite. Everything waking up again, starting fresh. It's full of possibility."

Angelica smiled. "I think that's why we work so well together. You're spring; I'm autumn. You look ahead; I reflect. And somehow, we meet in the middle."

John squeezed her hand gently, his voice softer now. "We always do."

They stopped outside his classroom, and for a moment, neither spoke.

"Don't ever stop telling me what you think," John said finally, his eyes steady on hers.

"And you don't ever stop reminding me to see the heart of things," Angelica replied.

As she turned to leave, she paused, looking back at him. "You know, John, you're not just like those trees out there. You're like spring itself—steady, full of hope, and always ready to start again."

Her words settled over him like sunlight breaking through a cloudy day. He watched her walk down the hall, her presence as steady and certain as the rhythm of the seasons.

John turned back to the door of his classroom, his heart lighter than before.

If Angelica was his autumn, he thought, then spring would always be their bridge—a place where love, respect, and growth flourished together.

Music Brings the Town Together

1964

The school gymnasium had never looked so alive. Rows of chairs filled every available space, and the walls were adorned with garlands of paper snowflakes, hand-painted banners, and twinkling lights that cast a warm glow over the gathering crowd. The scent of pine from a small cluster of decorated trees mingled with the aroma of coffee and baked goods brought by eager parents.

Angelica stood at the edge of the stage, her green dress catching the light as she surveyed the audience. Families, teachers, and townsfolk filled the room, their chatter creating a soft hum of anticipation. She held a clipboard tightly, but her confident smile betrayed none of the nervous energy she felt inside.

"Miss Thompson!" Bobby Ferillo's voice called out from behind her.

She turned to see the boy clutching his violin, his cheeks flushed. "I think the A string is too loose. Can you check it?"

Angelica crouched beside him, gently taking the instrument and inspecting it. "You're right. Let me tighten it just a bit. There—how does that feel?"

Bobby plucked the string and nodded. "Better. Thanks."

"You're going to be wonderful," Angelica said, resting a hand on his shoulder. "Just play like you did in rehearsal, and you'll be great."

Bobby grinned, though a flicker of nerves remained in his eyes.

As the lights dimmed, Angelica stepped to the microphone at the center of the stage. The audience quieted, all eyes turning to her.

"Good evening, everyone," she began, her voice steady despite the excitement buzzing in her chest. "Thank you all for joining us tonight. This concert is more than just a performance—it's a celebration of our school, our students, and the incredible community that supports us."

She gestured to the rows of students seated near the stage, their faces glowing with a mix of excitement and apprehension. "These young performers have worked hard over the past few months, and tonight, they're here to share their talents with all of you. I hope you'll give them your warmest encouragement as they take the stage."

The crowd applauded, and Angelica smiled, stepping aside to let the first group—a cheerful quartet of first-graders with tambourines—begin their act.

The performances unfolded smoothly, each group receiving cheers and applause from the audience. A second-grade choir sang *Twinkle, Twinkle, Little Star*, their small voices bright and sweet. Fifth-graders performed a playful skit about winter, drawing laughter and delight.

Then came the highlight of the evening: Bobby Ferillo's violin solo.

The gym fell silent as Bobby walked onto the stage, his violin tucked under his arm. He glanced toward Angelica, who gave him a reassuring nod from the wings. Taking a deep breath, he positioned the bow and began to play.

The first notes of *Ave Maria* floated through the air, hauntingly beautiful and achingly tender. The gym seemed to hold its breath, the melody weaving through the room and wrapping itself around the audience. Bobby's movements were steady, his focus unshakable as he poured his heart into each note.

In the wings, Angelica clasped her hands together, her eyes shimmering with pride. She had seen Bobby grow from a hesitant boy who barely dared to touch the keys of the piano into a confident young musician who could command a room with his playing.

When the final note hung in the air and slowly faded, the audience erupted into applause. Bobby lowered the violin, his face flushed, a small, proud smile breaking through his usual shyness.

John Anderson, seated near the back of the gym, found himself clapping harder than he'd intended. He looked around at the beaming faces of parents and townsfolk, the energy in the room unmistakable.

As the concert came to a close, Angelica returned to the microphone.

"Before we end tonight's program, I'd like to thank all the students for their hard work and courage, and all of you for supporting them. Events like this remind us of what makes our school and our town so special: the connections we share and the moments we create together."

She gestured to the students behind her. "And now, for our finale, we invite everyone to join us in singing *We Wish You a Merry Christmas*."

The children began singing, their voices joined by the audience as the festive melody filled the gym. Even John found himself humming along, a rare smile tugging at his lips.

Later, as the crowd filtered out and parents lingered to congratulate their children, John found Angelica near the piano, her arms full of sheet music. She was humming softly to herself, the same melody the children had sung earlier, her cheeks still flushed from the evening's success.

He leaned casually against the edge of the stage, watching her for a moment before speaking.

"That was something else," he said, his voice warm and familiar. "I think you might have pulled off a little miracle tonight."

Angelica looked up, her auburn hair falling loose from where she'd pinned it earlier. She smiled at him, that soft, knowing smile that always melted his resolve.

"It wasn't a miracle," she said, tucking a stray strand behind her ear. "Just a lot of practice and more than a few bribes with cookies."

John chuckled, crossing the space between them. "Don't sell yourself short, Angelica. You didn't just lead a concert—you brought the entire community together. That's something only you could do."

She paused in her stacking, her expression softening as she looked up at him. "Music has a way of doing that," she said thoughtfully. "It's not about perfect notes or flawless rhythms—it's about how it makes people feel. That's why I love it so much."

John reached out, brushing a speck of dust from her sleeve. "And that's why I love you so much. You don't just teach music. You teach people how to see the best in themselves."

Angelica's cheeks flushed deeper, and she laughed softly. "You're biased, John Anderson. But I'll take it."

He glanced around the gym, taking in the lingering parents, the scattered chairs, and the fading excitement of the evening.

"You know," he said, lowering his voice so only she could hear, "tonight wasn't just about the kids. You reminded all of us—myself included—what this school stands for. It's not just a place. It's a part of who we are."

Angelica reached for his hand, her fingers intertwining with his. "And you're part of why it's so special, John. You've given so much to this place—to everyone here. I hope you know that."

He tightened his grip on her hand, his voice softening. "I do. And I hope you know I couldn't have done it without you."

They stood there in a quiet bubble of shared understanding, the hum of the gym fading into the background. The concert was more than a success—it was a reminder of the traditions they cherished, the community they served, and the life they were building together.

Angelica leaned into him briefly, resting her head against his shoulder. "We make a good team, don't we?"

John kissed the top of her head, his voice full of affection. "The best."

The school had emptied by the time they gathered their things to leave. The night air outside was crisp and cool, and Angelica wrapped her arm around John's as they walked to the car.

"You know," she said thoughtfully, "this was the kind of night I dreamed about when I took this job. A room full of music, a group of children discovering something beautiful about themselves, and—" She hesitated, glancing up at him.

"And what?" he prompted, his lips quirking into a knowing smile.

"And you, standing there, looking at me like I'm the only person in the room," she finished, her voice barely above a whisper.

John stopped walking, turning to face her. He cupped her face gently in his hands, his gaze steady. "That's because you are, Angelica. Always."

She stood on tiptoe to kiss him, their shared warmth cutting through the coolness of the night.

But as they drove away, Angelica reached over to place a hand on John's arm.

"Let's not go home just yet," she said, her eyes glinting with mischief.

"It's late," he teased, glancing at her. "Aren't you tired?"

"I'm too happy to be tired," she replied. "And besides, I know just the place."

She directed him to a pullout by the lake, a spot they had stumbled upon years ago during one of their long drives. The water stretched out before them, still and dark, reflecting the starlit sky.

"Let's get out," she said, already opening her door.

Standing side by side, the cool breeze brushing against them, they looked out over the vast expanse of the lake. Angelica hugged herself, a thoughtful expression on her face.

"Do you ever think about where we'll be in ten years?" she asked, her voice quiet.

John slipped his arm around her shoulders, pulling her close. "I try not to think that far ahead. I like where we are now too much to rush it."

She laughed softly, leaning her head against his shoulder. "That's such a John thing to say."

"And what's an Angelica thing to say?" he countered.

"Something like... 'We should dream big, but live fully in the moment.'"

John chuckled, his breath warm against the cool night. "That does sound like you."

They stood there for a long while, the stillness of the lake reflected in the quiet between them. Finally, Angelica broke the silence. "Do you ever think about having children, John? About what that might look like for us?"

He turned to face her, his expression thoughtful. "I do. Sometimes I wonder what it would be like to see the world through a child's eyes again—to teach them, watch them grow."

Angelica smiled wistfully. "I think we'd make a good team. You with your steady hand and me with..."

"Your beautiful chaos," John finished, grinning.

She laughed, the sound echoing softly into the night. "Beautiful chaos, huh? I'll take that."

John leaned down to kiss her. "Whatever happens, Angelica, we'll make it work. Together."

The drive home was filled with easy conversation and shared laughter. By the time they arrived, the moon was high in the sky, bathing their house in soft, silvery light.

Inside, the warmth of their home embraced them. Angelica set her sheet music on the piano, her fingers lingering on the keys as she played a few soft notes.

John watched her from the doorway, his heart full.

"You know," he said, stepping closer, "nights like this remind me why I fell in love with you."

She turned, her smile gentle. "Because I'm stubborn and made you stay late at a concert?"

"No," he said, wrapping his arms around her. "Because you make every moment feel like a new beginning."

She rested her head against his chest, her voice soft. "I'm glad we're here, John. Together. Whatever comes next, we'll face it."

"And we'll do it with beautiful chaos," he teased, earning a playful swat on the arm.

That night, as they lay in bed, the conversation drifted back to children—the possibility of them, the joy they might bring, and the life they'd build around their laughter.

"Maybe someday," Angelica whispered, her hand in his.

"Maybe someday," John agreed, his voice full of hope.

Principal Anderson Has Entered the Chat

1965

The sound of muffled footsteps and the occasional burst of laughter filtered through the thin walls of the principal's office. John Anderson sat in one of the two chairs positioned in front of Principal Harrison's desk, his posture rigid. His hands rested on his knees, fingers drumming lightly in a rare display of nerves.

Harrison, ever methodical, flipped through a thick folder with a contemplative hum, his wire-rimmed glasses perched on the end of his nose. Finally, he closed the folder and leaned back in his chair, studying John with a faint smile.

"Well, John," Harrison began, his voice measured, "you've been with this school for, what, seven years now?"

"Eight," John corrected, his voice calm despite the faint tension in his chest.

"Eight," Harrison repeated, nodding. "In that time, you've shown remarkable dedication. Your classroom is one of the most disciplined and effective in the school. Students respect you. The parents trust you. And I can't tell you how many times the staff has come to me singing your praises."

John shifted slightly, unsure how to respond. "I appreciate that, sir. I just do my best."

"Your best," Harrison said with a chuckle, "has set a pretty high bar for the rest of us." He folded his hands on the desk and leaned forward. "Which is why I've recommended you as my replacement."

John blinked, his carefully maintained composure faltering for a moment. "Your replacement?"

Harrison nodded. "I'm retiring at the end of the school year. The board has already approved my request to appoint you as the next principal of Jane's School."

The words hung in the air, and for a moment, John wasn't sure what to say.

"Sir, I'm honored," he began, his voice steadying. "But... are you sure I'm the right choice? I've only been here a few years. There are other staff members with more experience."

Harrison waved a dismissive hand. "Experience is important, but so is leadership. And you, John, have shown time and again that you have what it takes to guide this school. You're steady, dependable, and you care about these children—not just their academics, but their futures."

John nodded slowly, the weight of the responsibility settling on his shoulders.

"I won't lie to you," Harrison continued. "Being principal isn't easy. There will be challenges—budget cuts, parent complaints, staff conflicts—but I have no doubt you're up to the task. The school needs someone like you, someone who values tradition but isn't afraid to face the realities of change."

John's thoughts flicked to the familiar halls of the school, the classrooms where he had spent countless hours nurturing young minds, the music room where Angelica had brought her transformative spirit. The school wasn't just a building to him; it was a community, a legacy.

"I'll do it," he said finally, his voice firm. "If you and the board think I'm the right person for the job, I won't let you down."

Harrison smiled, his expression warm. "I never thought you would. Congratulations, Principal Anderson."

Later that day, John found himself in the music room, as he so often did when he needed to think. Angelica sat at the piano, her fingers brushing the keys lightly as she played a soft, wandering melody.

She glanced up as he entered, her eyes lighting up. "There you are. I thought you might have gone home already."

John leaned against the doorframe, his hands in his pockets. "I needed a moment to think. Harrison called me into his office this afternoon."

"Oh?" Angelica asked, tilting her head. "What did he want?"

John stepped closer, the faintest smile tugging at his lips. "He's retiring at the end of the year. And he wants me to take his place."

Angelica's hands stilled on the keys, and she turned to face him fully. "John, that's wonderful! You'll make an incredible principal."

"You think so?" he asked, the faint hesitation in his tone betraying his usual confidence.

"I know so," she said, standing and crossing the room to him. She placed her hands gently on his arms. "You've always been the heart of this school. This is the right step, not just for you, but for everyone here. They trust you, and so do I."

John looked into her eyes, the weight of the decision feeling lighter under her gaze. "It's a lot of responsibility."

"You've carried that responsibility since the day you started teaching," Angelica said softly. "This just makes it official."

He nodded, the smile on his face growing. "I'll do my best."

"I know you will," she said with a grin. "And I'll be right here, every step of the way."

They stood together in the quiet music room, the sound of the piano's last notes fading into the stillness. It wasn't just a promotion—it was the next chapter in their shared journey, a promise to the school and to each other.

John and Angelica left the school hand in hand, the weight of the day replaced by a shared sense of accomplishment and quiet joy. The night was brisk, the spring air filled with the scent of fresh blossoms.

"I think tonight calls for a celebration," Angelica said as they reached the car, her auburn hair catching the soft glow of the streetlights.

"A celebration?" John asked, raising an eyebrow as he opened the passenger door for her.

"Something special," she said, sliding into the seat. "We deserve it, don't you think? You're practically the principal already, and the concert was a success. Let's not let the moment slip by."

John chuckled as he walked around to the driver's side. "Alright, Mrs. Anderson. Where to?"

"There's that little restaurant by the lake," Angelica suggested. "You know, the one we've been saying we should try for the last three years?"

"That's a bit of a splurge," John said, though his smile betrayed any real resistance.

Angelica reached over, taking his hand as he started the car. "Then it's perfect."

The restaurant was a cozy, candlelit haven overlooking the water, its windows reflecting the rippling lake and the star-filled sky above. They were seated by the window, the soft murmur of other diners creating a pleasant backdrop for their evening.

Angelica ordered a glass of wine, playfully insisting John try a sip even though he politely declined a glass of his own. The food was exquisite, each dish a reminder of how rare these indulgences were for them.

"This is nice," Angelica said, her voice warm as she swirled her wineglass. "A moment just for us."

John nodded, his hand resting on hers across the table. "It's been a good day."

She smiled, her expression turning thoughtful. "I'm proud of you, you know. For taking the principal job. It's a big step."

"I'm just hoping I don't let anyone down," he admitted, his tone candid.

"You won't," she said firmly, her thumb brushing his knuckles. "And even if things get hard, you'll have me. We're in this together, John."

"I know," he said, his voice quiet. "I couldn't do it without you."

On the drive home, Angelica leaned back in her seat, watching the dark silhouettes of the trees pass by the window. As they approached the lake, she sat up suddenly.

"Let's stop here," she said, pointing to a pullout just ahead.

John slowed the car, pulling into the spot. The lake stretched out before them, its surface shimmering under the moonlight.

Angelica stepped out, wrapping her scarf tighter around her neck as the cool breeze swept over them. John followed, his cane tapping softly on the ground.

"I love it here," she said, her voice almost a whisper. "It feels like the world pauses for a moment."

He stood beside her, his arm brushing hers as they gazed at the water. "You've always had a way of finding beauty in the quiet places."

She turned to him, her expression serious but tender. "Do you ever think about what's next for us, John? Beyond the school, beyond nights like this?"

He met her gaze, his brow furrowing slightly. "What do you mean?"

She hesitated, her eyes drifting back to the lake, its surface rippling gently in the moonlight. "I mean... whether we'll ever have a family of our own. Are you disappointed we haven't? That it hasn't happened yet?"

John's breath caught for a moment, the question settling heavily between them. He reached for her hand, his fingers warm against the coolness of hers. "Of course, I think about it," he said softly, his voice steady but filled with emotion. "But it's not something we can control. And honestly, Angelica, as long as I have you, I have everything I'll ever need."

Her eyes glistened, though she quickly blinked away the tears. "I feel the same. I just wonder sometimes... if we'll ever get to experience that part of life. To share what we've built with someone else."

He stepped closer, wrapping his arms around her. "If it happens, it happens. And if it doesn't, we'll still have this. Us. The life we've made together."

She rested her head against his chest, her voice barely audible. "You always know just what to say."

"And you always remind me what matters," he replied, kissing her.

When they arrived home, the house felt especially warm and welcoming. Angelica slipped off her scarf, placing it neatly by the door before moving to the piano. She played a few soft chords, the familiar melody of her favorite song filling the room.

John sat nearby, watching her, his heart full. "You always end the night with music," he said.

"And you always listen," she replied, smiling.

Later, as they settled into bed, the conversation from the lake resurfaced.

"Do you think we'd make good parents?" Angelica asked, her voice thoughtful.

"I think we'd make great parents," John said, turning to face her. "But I also think we've made a difference in so many children's lives already. That's no small thing, Angelica."

She reached for his hand, intertwining their fingers. "No, it's not. But it's good to dream, isn't it?"

He smiled, kissing her hand. "It is. And whatever dreams come true, we'll face them together."

Summer Serenades

1966

The cicadas droned in the late afternoon heat, their steady hum blending with the faint sound of children's laughter coming from the music room. Outside, the schoolyard lay still, the playground deserted under the blazing sun. Most of the town's children were at home or at the lake, escaping the oppressive warmth of a July day.

But inside Jane's School, the music room was alive with sound.

Angelica stood at the piano, her green summer dress catching the occasional breeze from the lone oscillating fan positioned in the corner. A small group of children sat on benches around her, their faces intent as they watched her hands glide across the keys.

"Okay, everyone," Angelica said, turning to the children with a bright smile. "Let's go over that one more time. Remember, it's not just about hitting the right notes—it's about feeling the music. Let it come from here." She tapped her chest gently.

A boy in the back, Danny, raised his hand tentatively. "Miss Thompson, what if we hit the wrong note again?"

Angelica's smile softened. "Then you keep going, Danny. Mistakes are just part of learning. The important thing is that you don't stop. Music is about persistence and heart, not perfection."

The children nodded, and she resumed her place at the piano. As her fingers danced over the keys, the students joined in with their recorders, flutes, and a single battered guitar held by a girl named Maria. The sound wasn't perfect, but it was earnest, and Angelica's encouragement wove through the notes like an unspoken harmony.

Later, as the children packed up their instruments, a boy lingered near the door. His name was Jimmy, a quiet child whose family struggled to make ends meet. Angelica noticed his hesitation and walked over, crouching slightly to meet his eye level.

"Something on your mind, Jimmy?" she asked gently.

Jimmy hesitated, then mumbled, "My mom says I shouldn't bother you too much. She says we can't afford for me to do this for long."

Angelica's heart ached at his words. She placed a hand on his shoulder. "Jimmy, listen to me. These lessons are my gift to you and the others. There's no cost, no strings attached. You're not bothering me—you're inspiring me."

Jimmy's eyes widened. "Really?"

"Really," she said firmly. "You have talent, Jimmy. Don't let anything stop you from exploring it. You belong here just as much as anyone else."

He nodded, a small smile breaking across his face. "Thank you, Miss Thompson."

"You're very welcome. Now, go home and practice what we learned today. I want to hear how much you've improved by next week."

As the last of the children left, the room fell quiet. Angelica began tidying up, collecting sheet music and arranging chairs.

John appeared in the doorway, his shirt sleeves rolled up, his usual stern expression softened by a faint smile. "You're still at it," he said.

Angelica looked up, brushing a strand of hair from her face. "And I will be all summer."

"You're not getting paid for this, you know," John pointed out, though his tone carried no real reproach.

"I know," she replied with a shrug. "But some of these kids don't get opportunities like this. If I can give them even a little bit of what music gave me, it's worth every minute."

John stepped into the room, his hands in his pockets. "You're remarkable, Angelica. I hope you know that."

She laughed lightly, shaking her head. "I'm just doing what feels right. These kids deserve a chance to shine."

He leaned against the piano, watching her with quiet admiration. "You're making a difference. More than you realize."

Angelica smiled, her gaze lingering on him for a moment before she returned to her tidying. "Well, someone has to keep up with you, Principal Anderson. I hear you're a tough act to follow."

John chuckled, shaking his head. "I think you're setting the bar for both of us."

The sun dipped lower in the sky, casting long shadows across the music room as Angelica locked up for the evening. The summer air was still hot, but she didn't mind.

The children's laughter and the echoes of their music followed her as she walked to her car, a sense of purpose and fulfillment filling her chest. She knew the lessons she was giving weren't just about music—they were about hope, confidence, and showing these kids that their voices mattered.

And that, she thought, was worth everything.

The next day dawned with the promise of company, the kind that Angelica and John seldom received. Her brother, Edward, was driving up from Indiana with his wife, Clara, and their two children, a boy of seven and a girl of five—James and Nichole. It was a rare occasion; the distance between them often made visits infrequent, but the arrival was always cherished.

By mid-morning, the house was abuzz with preparations. Angelica moved through the kitchen, a lightness in her step as she prepared a batch of cookies while John set up the extra bedding in the guest room.

"They'll be here soon," Angelica said, glancing at the clock. "Do you think we have enough for lunch?"

John leaned against the doorframe, his sleeves rolled up and a faint smile on his face. "Angelica, you've made enough food to feed the entire school board. Twice."

She laughed, swatting playfully at him with a dish towel. "Well, I don't want them to think we're unprepared."

"You're the most prepared person I know," John said, his tone affectionate. "Ed's lucky to have you as a sister."

"And you as a brother-in-law," Angelica added, giving him a warm smile. "You've been so good to him, all of them, John."

The sound of tires crunching on the gravel drive drew their attention. Angelica dashed to the front door, flinging it open just as Edward stepped out of the car.

"Ed!" she called, her voice bright with excitement.

"Angie!" Edward grinned, pulling her into a tight hug as soon as he reached the steps. "It's good to see you."

Behind him, Clara helped the children out of the car. James waved shyly, while Emily clung to her mother's hand.

John joined Angelica on the porch, shaking Edward's hand firmly before turning to Clara. "Welcome back," he said warmly. "It's been too long."

"Far too long," Clara agreed, her smile kind. "But we're finally here."

The afternoon was spent in the backyard, the smell of grilled chicken wafting through the air as John manned the barbecue. James and Nichole chased each other across the lawn, their laughter blending with the chirping of crickets.

Angelica sat with Clara and Edward at the picnic table, a pitcher of lemonade between them.

"You two really have built a lovely life here," Edward said, gesturing to the house and garden.

"We've worked hard for it," Angelica replied, her gaze softening as she watched John flip the chicken with practiced ease. "But it's the people in our lives who make it truly special."

Clara tilted her head, her tone curious. "And you're both still teaching?"

"I'm the principal now," John said, setting a platter of chicken on the table. "But Angelica is the one with all the magic. She's been running free music lessons all summer for the kids in town."

"That's incredible," Edward said, his admiration clear. "You've always had a gift for connecting with people, Angie."

Angelica shrugged, though her cheeks pinkened. "It's just something I love. These kids deserve every chance they can get."

Later, as James and Nichole roasted marshmallows over a small fire pit, Angelica and Clara talked quietly while Edward joined John near the garden.

"She's amazing," Edward said, nodding toward his sister. "You know that, right?"

John chuckled. "I remind her every day. But she's too modest to believe me."

Edward's tone turned serious. "You two are good together. I see it. And I know things haven't been easy, with…" He trailed off, glancing toward the children.

John nodded, understanding. "We've had our moments of doubt. But Angelica's strength—it keeps me grounded. I'd like to think I do the same for her."

"You do," Edward said firmly. "I can see it."

That night, after little James and Nichole had been tucked into the guest room and Edward and Clara had retired for the night, Angelica and John found themselves sitting on the porch swing, the night air cool and comforting.

"Today was nice," Angelica said softly, leaning into John's shoulder.

"It was," he agreed. "It's good to see your brother. The kids seem happy."

Angelica nodded, her gaze drifting to the stars. "I know you still think about it… About what it would be like if we had children of our own?"

John exhaled, wrapping an arm around her. "I think about it sometimes. But I try not to dwell. What we have—it's more than I ever hoped for."

"I feel the same," Angelica said, her voice tinged with emotion. "But it's hard not to wonder."

John pressed a kiss to her lips. "I know. And if it happens, it happens. But if it doesn't, Angelica, I don't want you to ever feel like our life is anything less than full. Because it's not."

Her eyes glistened as she turned to him. "I don't. You've made me so happy, John. I just—sometimes I wonder if I've given you enough."

John's expression softened, his voice steady. "You've given me everything, Angelica. More than I ever thought I'd have."

She rested her head against his chest, the steady rhythm of his heartbeat grounding her.

"Together," she murmured, her voice full of quiet conviction.

As the night deepened, they sat in companionable silence, the love between them as enduring and steadfast as the stars above.

Living in a Shadow

1967

The late afternoon sun slanted through the windows of the Ferillo living room, casting long golden streaks across the worn rug and threadbare furniture. Tom sat on the floor, a pencil clutched in his hand as he hunched over his homework. Beside him on the couch, his older brother Bobby leaned back with an air of practiced ease, flipping through sheet music.

The soft, lilting notes of *Moonlight Sonata* drifted from the record player in the corner, a faint accompaniment to the tension hanging in the air.

"You almost done with that math, Tom?" Bobby asked, his voice casual but carrying the unmistakable tone of an older sibling's impatience.

"Almost," Tom mumbled, not looking up. His pencil scratched furiously at the paper, erasing mistakes as quickly as they appeared.

Bobby chuckled lightly. "You know, you'd finish a lot faster if you just focused."

"I am focused," Tom snapped, immediately regretting the sharpness in his tone. He glanced up, his cheeks flushing. "Sorry."

Bobby waved it off, his attention already back on the sheet music. "It's fine. Just saying, you make it harder than it needs to be."

Tom clenched his jaw but said nothing.

After dinner, the Ferillo household came alive with music, as it often did. Bobby sat at the family's upright piano, his fingers gliding effortlessly across the keys as he practiced one of Angelica's more advanced arrangements. Their parents sat nearby, their faces glowing with pride as they listened.

Tom lingered in the doorway, watching silently.

"That's beautiful, Bobby," their mother said, clapping lightly as the piece came to an end.

"Thanks, Mom," Bobby replied with an easy grin. "Miss Thompson says I might be ready for a recital soon."

"I'm sure you'll do wonderfully," their father said, his voice brimming with pride. "You've got a gift, son. Always have."

Tom shifted his weight, his fists tightening at his sides. He didn't begrudge Bobby his talent—it wasn't his fault he was good at everything. But no matter what Tom did, it felt like he was always standing in Bobby's shadow, unnoticed and unremarkable.

"Tom!" his father called, noticing him for the first time. "Come in here. What's got you hanging around the door like that?"

Tom hesitated, then stepped into the room, his head ducked slightly. "Just listening."

"Well, don't just listen," his mother said with a kind smile. "Why don't you play something?"

"Yeah, Tom," Bobby said, his tone teasing but not unkind. "Let's see what you've got."

"I don't play the piano," Tom muttered, his cheeks flushing.

"You could," Bobby said with a shrug. "It's not that hard. Miss Thompson could probably teach you a few things."

The words stung, though Bobby likely didn't mean them to. Tom shook his head. "I don't have time for that. Got too much homework."

"Well, don't let it pile up," their father said. "You've got a brain, Tom. You just need to use it."

Tom nodded, forcing a small smile. "Yeah, I know."

Later that evening, Tom sat alone in the room he shared with Bobby. The hum of conversation from the living room filtered in faintly, but he barely noticed. He stared at the math homework spread out before him, the numbers blurring together as his thoughts churned.

No matter what he did, he felt like he would always be second best. Bobby was the golden child—the talented musician, the natural leader, the one everyone noticed. Tom was just… there.

He sighed, dropping the pencil and rubbing his eyes.

The door creaked open, and Bobby stepped in, carrying a cup of water. "You still at it?"

Tom nodded, not looking up.

Bobby set the cup on the bedside table and sat on the edge of his bed. "Hey, you're doing fine, you know. Math's not my thing either."

Tom glanced at him, surprised. "You? You're good at everything."

Bobby laughed. "Not true. I bombed history last year, remember? Miss Thompson said I should stick to the piano and leave the dates to someone else."

Tom cracked a small smile despite himself. "Yeah, but you're still good at most stuff."

Bobby shrugged. "Maybe. But that doesn't mean you're not, too. You've got other stuff going for you, Tom."

"Like what?" Tom asked, his tone tinged with frustration.

"I don't know," Bobby said, leaning back against the wall. "You're good with people. And you don't quit, even when things are hard. That's something."

Tom's lips twitched into a half-smile, though doubt still lingered.

Bobby stood, ruffling Tom's hair as he passed. "You'll figure it out, little brother. Just don't be so hard on yourself."

As the door clicked shut, Tom stared down at his homework again. Bobby's words were kind, but they didn't erase the weight of always feeling like he had something to prove.

Someday, he thought, he'd find his place. Someday, he wouldn't feel like just "Bobby's brother." But tonight, that day felt far away.

Storm Clouds and Silver Linings

1968

The wind howled through the night, rattling the windows of Jane's School and sending loose branches tumbling across the playground. Thunder cracked loudly, shaking the panes, and flashes of lightning illuminated the empty halls for brief, eerie moments.

John Anderson stood in his modest office, his arms crossed tightly over his chest as he watched the storm rage through the window. Rain lashed against the glass, cascading in relentless sheets that turned the schoolyard into a small lake.

"It's holding," he muttered to himself, though the strain in his voice betrayed his concern.

The building was old, built long before modern construction standards, and while it had weathered many storms, tonight's ferocity was something different.

A sudden knock at the door startled him. He turned to see Angelica, her hair damp from her dash through the hall, peeking in.

"John, you're still here?" she asked, stepping inside.

"I could ask you the same thing," he replied.

Angelica shrugged, brushing droplets off her shoulders. "I stayed late with Bobby. He wanted to practice for his recital."

John glanced at the window again, the lightning revealing the silhouette of the flagpole outside. "You should head home. This storm's only getting worse."

"I was about to, but I thought I'd check on you first." She followed his gaze to the window. "You're worried about the building, aren't you?"

"It's seen better days," John admitted. "I've been meaning to request some maintenance funds, but…"

Another clap of thunder interrupted him, shaking the very floor beneath their feet.

The next morning, John arrived early to assess the damage. The storm had passed, leaving a gray sky streaked with hints of sunrise. But as he stepped out of his car, his stomach sank.

The roof of the gymnasium had suffered significant damage—large sections of shingles were missing, and part of the wooden frame was exposed. The flagpole, which had stood proudly at the front of the school for decades, leaned at a precarious angle, its base uprooted by the violent winds.

Water pooled around the building's foundation, and scattered debris littered the playground: twisted branches, chunks of roofing, and a stray basketball that had somehow made its way into the mud.

John sighed, running a hand over his face.

"John!"

He turned to see Angelica hurrying toward him, her boots splashing through the puddles. She carried a clipboard tucked under one arm.

"It's worse than I thought," she said, surveying the scene.

"Not irreparable," John replied, though his tone lacked conviction. "But it'll take time and money—two things we're always short on."

"We'll manage," Angelica said, her optimism unwavering. "We always do."

By midday, the staff had gathered to discuss the repairs. The teachers' lounge buzzed with concerned voices as John outlined the damage and the steps required to address it.

"The roof and the flagpole are our biggest priorities," John said, pointing to a hastily drawn sketch of the building. "We'll need to get quotes from contractors immediately. I'll be submitting a request to the school board for emergency funds, but we may also need to organize some fundraising efforts."

"Fundraising?" Cleary scoffed, crossing his arms. "How much more can we ask from the community? They've already got enough on their plates."

"It's not ideal," John admitted, "but this storm didn't give us much choice."

Angelica leaned forward, her brow furrowed. "Maybe we could organize an event—a concert, a fair, something to bring people together and raise what we need. We've done it before."

John nodded thoughtfully. "That's a possibility. Let's keep it on the table."

He paused, glancing around the room. "But it's not just about raising money, is it? This is bigger than that."

Rising from his seat, John moved to the window, his hands clasped behind his back. The view outside was bleak, the playground slick with rainwater and strewn with debris from the storm.

"Whatever we do," he said, his voice steady, "we need to focus on more than just repairs. This storm has reminded us of something important—how much this school means to everyone here. It's not just a building. It's a part of this town's history, and we have to treat it that way."

The room fell quiet, the weight of his words settling over the staff. Each face reflected a mix of resolve and reverence, their shared connection to the school silently reaffirmed.

Over the next few weeks, the school became a hive of activity. Contractors came and went, their trucks parked alongside the playground as workers patched the gymnasium roof and reinforced the weakened foundation.

True to her word, Angelica spearheaded a fundraising concert, enlisting students, parents, and even local businesses to help. The event drew a crowd that filled the gymnasium to capacity, raising enough to cover some of the costs the school board couldn't.

Through it all, the resilience of Jane's School became evident. Parents volunteered their time, students helped clean up the playground, and staff worked tirelessly to ensure classes continued uninterrupted.

One afternoon, as the repairs neared completion, John stood outside, watching workers install a new flagpole. The polished steel gleamed in the sunlight, a symbol of the school's endurance.

Angelica joined him, her hands clasped behind her back. "It's starting to feel like home again," she said.

"It never stopped being home," John replied, a faint smile on his lips.

She looked at him, her expression warm. "You're right. This place has been through a lot, but it always comes back stronger. Just like the people in it."

John nodded, his gaze fixed on the flagpole as it was raised into place. "Resilience," he said quietly. "That's what this school is built on."

The flag unfurled in the breeze, its colors vibrant against the clear blue sky. The storm had left its mark, but it had also reinforced something unshakable— the spirit of the school and the community that rallied around it.

Later that week, as the contractors packed up their tools and the final repairs were completed, the flurry of activity around Jane's School began to settle. John felt a familiar weight lift from his shoulders, but another remained. He had been preoccupied—distant, even—and he knew Angelica had noticed. She always did.

He had been determined to keep the school running smoothly, but in the process, he'd let something slip: the little moments that made their life together special. That evening, he decided to make it right.

"Put on something nice," John said as Angelica stood in the kitchen, sorting through mail.

She raised an eyebrow, looking up at him with playful suspicion. "Why? Are we expecting someone?"

"No," he said, his tone measured but warm. "We're going out."

Angelica set the stack of envelopes aside, crossing her arms. "John Anderson, are you taking me on a date?"

"That's the idea," he replied, his lips twitching into a faint smile.

She studied him for a moment before nodding. "Alright, then. Give me fifteen minutes."

The restaurant he chose was one of the nicest in town, a place they rarely visited except on special occasions. Candlelight flickered on white tablecloths, and soft music played in the background. As they were seated near a window overlooking the quiet street, Angelica tilted her head, her auburn hair catching the golden glow of the lights.

"This feels like a celebration," she said, her voice soft.

"It is," John replied, unfolding his napkin. "The repairs are done, the school is whole again. That's worth celebrating."

She gave him a knowing look. "And what else?"

He hesitated, his hands resting on the edge of the table. "And us," he said finally, his voice quieter. "I haven't exactly been the best company these past few weeks. You deserved better than that."

Angelica reached across the table, taking his hand in hers. "You've had a lot on your plate, John. I know how much this school means to you."

"And you mean just as much to me," he said, his gaze steady. "I might not always show it when I get caught up in everything else, but I hope you know."

Her expression softened, and she squeezed his hand. "I do. And I've never doubted it."

They sat in comfortable silence for a moment, the unspoken understanding between them filling the space.

The meal was unhurried, each course a reminder of how rare and cherished these moments were. Angelica laughed as John recounted Cleary's dramatic reaction to the storm repairs, and John smiled as Angelica described how one of her students, Jimmy, had worked up the courage to perform a solo at the fundraising concert.

"It's not just the school that's resilient," she said, sipping her wine. "It's the people in it. The kids, the parents, the staff. You see that, don't you?"

"I do," John said, nodding. "And I think it's why we do what we do. This place—this community—it's worth fighting for."

Her eyes glimmered with pride. "You're part of what makes it worth fighting for, John. The children see it, the staff sees it, and so does the town."

He leaned back slightly, a rare moment of vulnerability crossing his face. "It's a lot to live up to."

"You don't have to live up to anything," Angelica said, her voice firm but gentle. "You just have to be you. That's always been enough."

As they left the restaurant, Angelica laced her arm through John's. "This was lovely," she said, her voice full of contentment.

"It's not over yet," he said, steering her toward the car.

She gave him a curious look but said nothing, letting him take the lead.

John drove them to the edge of town, where the road wrapped around the lake. He parked at a pullout overlooking the water, the moonlight reflecting off the rippling surface.

Angelica stepped out, pulling her coat tighter against the cool breeze. "You know, you've been bringing me to this lake for years, and it never gets old."

"It's peaceful," John said, joining her by the railing.

"And romantic," she added, her eyes dancing as she glanced at him.

He smiled faintly, resting his hand on hers where it lay on the cool metal. "I thought it was time to remind you that I haven't forgotten what's important."

She turned to face him fully, her expression tender. "You don't have to remind me, John. I see it in everything you do."

They stood together for a long moment, the quiet night wrapping around them like a blanket.

As they drove home, Angelica reached for his hand, intertwining her fingers with his. "You're not so bad at this romance thing, Principal Anderson," she teased.

"Well," he said with mock seriousness, "I like to think I can surprise you now and then."

Back at the house, Angelica made tea while John settled into his armchair, the glow of the fireplace casting warm shadows across the room.

"Do you think we'll always be like this?" she asked as she handed him a mug, sitting beside him on the couch.

"Like what?" he asked, raising an eyebrow.

"Finding our way back to each other, no matter what's happening around us."

He reached for her hand, his voice steady. "Always."

Angelica smiled, leaning against his shoulder. The storm outside was long gone, but in its wake, it had left something stronger: their shared resilience and the quiet certainty that, together, they could weather anything.

A Quiet Evening at Home

1969

The hum of the ceiling fan filled the living room, blending with the soft crackle of the radio. Outside, crickets chirped in a symphony of summer night sounds, the world settling into its quiet rhythm. The house felt warm and lived-in, the kind of comfort that came with years of shared routines and unspoken understandings.

John sat in his armchair, his reading glasses perched low on his nose, staring blankly at the open book on his lap. Across the room, Angelica lounged on the couch, her legs tucked beneath her as she absentmindedly flipped through a magazine. The evening should have felt peaceful, but there was something unspoken in the air, a quiet tension neither had yet named.

"You've been staring at that page for ten minutes," Angelica said gently, glancing up from her magazine.

John sighed, setting the book aside and rubbing his temples. "It's not exactly captivating reading," he replied, though they both knew that wasn't the reason for his distraction.

Angelica set her magazine down and crossed the room to him, sitting on the arm of his chair. "All right, John. What is it? What's eating at you?"

He hesitated, his hands resting on his knees. "It's the school," he admitted finally. "It's not just the building this time. It's everything else—the staff, the board, the direction things are going."

Angelica tilted her head. "What do you mean?"

John's brow furrowed, his voice tinged with frustration. "There's pressure to make changes—cut costs, merge programs, even reduce staff hours. They're calling it modernization, but all I see is a loss of what makes the school special. What we've worked so hard to build."

Angelica nodded slowly. "It sounds like they're asking you to make sacrifices that don't sit right with you."

"They're asking all of us to make sacrifices," John said, his voice quieter now. "And I hate that I'm the one who has to decide where to draw the line."

Angelica slid off the arm of the chair and knelt beside him, her green eyes searching his face. "You've always made decisions that put the children and the community first, John. That's why the staff respects you, why the parents trust you. You've earned that trust."

John looked at her, the tension in his expression softening. "But what if it's not enough? What if I make the wrong call and the school loses what makes it special?"

"You won't," she said firmly. "Because you care too much to let that happen. And you're not in this alone."

He reached out, brushing a strand of hair from her face. "I don't tell you enough how much I lean on you, Angelica. How much I need you."

Her lips curved into a small smile. "I know. But it's nice to hear every now and then."

The quiet stretched between them, not uncomfortable but heavy with thought. Angelica broke it first, her tone lighter now. "You know what I think we need?"

John raised an eyebrow. "What's that?"

"A break," she said, standing and stretching. "A weekend away. Just you and me, somewhere quiet. No meetings, no school talk, no debates about modernization. Just us."

"A whole weekend?" he asked, his tone skeptical but amused.

"Yes," she said, placing her hands on her hips. "A whole weekend. You can't keep running on fumes, John. And I refuse to let you burn out."

He chuckled softly, shaking his head. "You're relentless."

"And you love me for it," she teased, leaning down to kiss his cheek.

"That I do," he replied, his voice tender. "All right, Angelica. You win. We'll take a weekend—just the two of us."

Later that evening, after the lights were dimmed and the house had settled into its nighttime stillness, they lay side by side in bed. Angelica reached for John's hand under the covers, their fingers intertwining.

"You know," she said softly, "I've been thinking about what you said. About the school losing what makes it special."

"What about it?" he asked, his voice low in the dark.

"I don't think it's the school itself that makes it special," she said. "It's the people. The memories. The moments we create there. Those can't be taken away by budget cuts or modernization."

John was quiet for a moment, her words settling into him like stones in a stream. "You're right," he said finally. "It's the people. And as long as we hold onto that, nothing can really change what matters."

Angelica smiled, her head resting on his shoulder. "You see? You already have the answer, John. You just needed to say it out loud."

He kissed the top of her head, his arm tightening around her. "I don't know what I'd do without you, Angelica."

"Luckily," she said, her voice light with a touch of humor, "you'll never have to find out."

The following Friday afternoon, John loaded the last of their bags into the car while Angelica stood on the porch, locking the front door. She wore a light sundress that fluttered in the gentle breeze, a wide-brimmed hat shielding her face from the summer sun.

"You look like you're ready for an adventure," John said, his tone warm as she walked toward him.

She laughed, slipping her hand into his. "After the past few months, I think we've earned one. Are you sure you can leave everything behind for a couple of days?"

"Positive," he replied, opening the passenger door for her. "Cleary has the staff under control, the school board won't meet until Monday, and my desk is as clear as it's ever going to get."

"Well then," Angelica said, settling into her seat. "Let's go before you change your mind."

John chuckled as he climbed into the driver's seat and started the engine. "You're in charge this weekend, Mrs. Anderson. Where are we headed first?"

They drove out of town, the familiar landscape giving way to rolling hills and thick, green forests. The air felt lighter the farther they went, the worries of home fading with each passing mile.

By early evening, they arrived at a small lakeside cabin Angelica had found through a friend. It was simple but charming, with a wraparound porch and a view of the water that stretched endlessly beneath the setting sun.

"This is perfect," Angelica said, stepping out of the car and taking a deep breath. "You can almost hear the quiet."

John joined her, his hands on his hips as he surveyed the scene. "Almost. But I think I hear something else."

"What's that?"

"The sound of you proving me wrong all weekend," he teased.

Angelica grinned, swatting his arm playfully. "You'll thank me for this, John Anderson. Just wait."

After unpacking and a simple dinner of sandwiches and fresh fruit on the porch, the two settled into a pair of rocking chairs, a bottle of wine between them. The lake shimmered in the moonlight, the sound of lapping waves a soothing rhythm against the quiet of the evening.

Angelica leaned back, her head tilted toward the sky. "Look at all those stars," she said softly. "It feels like you could reach out and touch them."

John glanced up, his eyes reflecting the starlight. "You don't see skies like this back in town."

"That's because you're always too busy to look," she teased, her tone light.

He smiled, reaching over to take her hand. "You're right. I don't look enough. At the stars, or at you."

Her eyes softened as she turned to him. "You're looking now."

"I am," he said, his voice quiet but steady. "And I'm thinking about how lucky I am."

Angelica squeezed his hand, her lips curving into a smile. "So am I."

The sun rose early, casting golden light across the lake. Angelica woke first, slipping out to the porch with a cup of coffee. She was halfway through her second cup when John joined her, still groggy but smiling.

"What's on the agenda today?" he asked, leaning against the porch railing.

"Nothing," Angelica said, grinning at his puzzled expression.

"Nothing?"

"Absolutely nothing. No schedules, no plans. We'll do whatever we feel like doing."

John chuckled, shaking his head. "You're going to drive me crazy with this."

"You love it," she replied, handing him his coffee.

They spent the day walking along the lake, skipping stones across its surface, and reading quietly together under the shade of a towering oak tree. Angelica coaxed John into a short canoe ride, and though he grumbled about the unsteadiness of the boat, he couldn't help but smile at her delight.

When the sun was high, they stopped for a picnic lunch on a small grassy hill overlooking the water. Angelica stretched out on the blanket, her head resting on John's lap as they talked about everything and nothing.

"This," John said after a while, his voice thoughtful. "This is what I didn't know I needed."

Angelica looked up at him, her eyes warm. "I knew you'd come around."

That night, after a simple dinner and another quiet moment on the porch, John and Angelica sat by the fireplace in the cabin's small living room. The flickering flames cast a warm glow over the room as they shared stories from their early days at the school.

"Do you remember your first week there?" Angelica asked, her voice teasing. "You were so serious."

"I was trying to make a good impression," John replied, chuckling. "And you were playing that piano loud enough to rattle the walls."

"That was my way of making a good impression," she quipped, laughing.

John leaned back in his chair, his expression softening. "You've always been good at that—making an impression. On me, on the students, on the community. I don't think you realize just how much of a difference you've made."

Angelica reached across the small table between them, her hand finding his. "I think I do," she said softly. "Because I've seen the difference you've made, John. And I've been lucky enough to share it with you."

As the fire burned low and the night deepened, they found themselves curled together on the couch, the warmth of their love wrapping around them as surely as the quilt Angelica had pulled over their laps.

"This was a good idea," John murmured, his voice heavy with contentment.

Angelica smiled against his shoulder. "You're welcome."

"I should let you make the plans more often," he added, his lips twitching into a faint smile.

"Don't push your luck, Principal Anderson," she teased, her voice filled with laughter and love.

And in the quiet cabin by the lake, with the stars shining brightly above, they let the rest of the world fade away, content in the simple joy of being together.

Goodbye, Bobby, Hello World

1970

The morning was crisp and bright, the kind of late summer day that hinted at the coming autumn. The Ferillo family stood clustered near the idling bus at the edge of the town square. A small suitcase rested at Bobby's feet, its corners scuffed from years of use.

Angelica and John had come to see him off, standing alongside Bobby's parents and his younger brother, Tom. The mood was heavy with the weight of goodbyes, but there was also an undercurrent of pride—Bobby Ferillo, the boy who had first timidly tapped out melodies on the school piano, was leaving for college on a full music scholarship.

"Do you have everything, Bobby?" Mrs. Ferillo asked, her voice trembling.

"Yes, Mom," Bobby said gently, his confident tone masking his own nerves.

"And you'll write?"

"Of course."

Angelica stepped forward, her smile warm but tinged with emotion. "Bobby, I want you to know how proud I am of you. You've worked so hard for this, and you've earned every bit of it."

Bobby's composure wavered for a moment, and he gave her a shy smile. "Thank you, Miss Thompson. I wouldn't be here without you."

She reached out, pulling him into a hug. "You got here because of your own talent and determination. Don't ever forget that."

When she stepped back, John approached, his hand extended. Bobby shook it firmly, his grip strong but respectful.

"You're going to do great things, Bobby," John said, his voice steady. "We'll miss you around here, but we know you'll make us proud."

"I'll do my best, Mr. Anderson," Bobby replied.

Tom, standing off to the side, looked down at his sneakers, his hands jammed into his pockets. Bobby turned to him, his expression softening.

"Take care of Mom and Dad, all right?" Bobby said, clapping a hand on his younger brother's shoulder.

Tom nodded, his voice barely above a whisper. "I will."

The bus driver leaned out of the door, his voice cutting through the moment. "All aboard! We've got a schedule to keep!"

Bobby picked up his suitcase, hesitating for a moment before stepping onto the bus. He paused in the doorway, turning to look at the group one last time.

"I'll be back for the holidays," he said, though it sounded more like a promise to himself than to anyone else.

"We'll be here," Mrs. Ferillo said, her hand clutching her husband's arm.

The bus door closed with a soft hiss, and the engine roared as it pulled away from the curb. Everyone waved, their eyes following the bus until it disappeared down the road.

Later that afternoon, Angelica and John sat on the bench beneath the great maples outside the school. The branches swayed gently in the breeze, their leaves just beginning to turn.

"Feels like the end of an era," Angelica said, her hands folded in her lap.

"It does," John agreed, his gaze fixed on the horizon.

"He was one of the special ones," Angelica continued, her voice soft. "Not just because of his talent, but because of his heart. Watching him grow, seeing him find his confidence—it's why I became a teacher."

John nodded, his tone reflective. "You gave him something that will stay with him forever. And he'll carry that wherever he goes."

"And so will we," Angelica said with a small smile.

They sat in companionable silence, the sounds of the town fading into the background. It was a bittersweet moment—a goodbye to a chapter of their lives, but also a reminder of the impact they had made together.

As the sun dipped lower in the sky, Angelica reached for John's hand, intertwining her fingers with his. They didn't need words to convey what they were feeling. The departure of Bobby Ferillo wasn't just a goodbye—it was a testament to the work they had poured into their lives, their school, and their community.

And in that quiet moment, they knew their efforts had been worth it.

The Nam Calls Bobby

1971

The news arrived on a gray, overcast morning, carried in a slim envelope with official lettering on the front. Bobby Ferillo sat at the kitchen table of his family's modest home, the letter open in his trembling hands. Across from him, his mother stared at the words as if willing them to change, her face pale and tight.

His father stood behind her, one hand on her shoulder, the other clenched into a fist at his side. "The draft," Mr. Ferillo muttered, his voice low and bitter. "They got him."

Tom sat on the edge of the couch in the adjoining room, silent and still, his usual fidgeting stilled by the gravity of the moment.

"Mom, Dad, it'll be all right," Bobby said, his voice steady but thin. "I'll do my duty. They'll train me. I'll—"

"You shouldn't have to," Mrs. Ferillo said sharply, her voice cracking. She reached out, gripping his hand tightly. "You're a musician, not a soldier."

"They don't care about that," Mr. Ferillo said, his tone hard but his eyes wet.

The news spread quickly through the town, carried by whispers in the market and murmurs in the school halls. Bobby Ferillo—one of Jane's School's brightest stars, the young musician who had earned a college scholarship—was being sent to war.

At school, Angelica sat at her desk in the music room, staring at the piano. Her sheet music lay untouched beside her, her hands clasped tightly in her lap. When John entered the room, she didn't look up.

"I heard," John said softly, closing the door behind him.

Angelica nodded, her jaw set. "It's not fair, John. He's just a boy. He has his whole life ahead of him—concerts, compositions, everything he's worked for—and now..." She trailed off, shaking her head.

John crossed the room and sat on the bench beside her. "This war has taken too much already. And now it's taking one of our own."

Angelica turned to him, her green eyes shining with unshed tears. "What do we do? How do we help him?"

John placed a reassuring hand on her shoulder. "We do what we've always done. We support him, and we support his family. And we make sure he knows that no matter what happens, this community will be here for him."

At a town meeting held that evening in the school gymnasium, concerned parents, neighbors, and former students gathered to talk about the draft and its growing impact on their small town.

Mayor Richards stood at the front of the room, his expression heavy as he looked out over the gathered crowd. The town hall was unusually full, with families packed shoulder to shoulder, their whispered conversations barely masking the undercurrent of worry and grief.

"We've had several of our boys drafted over the past years," he began, his voice steady but weighted with emotion, "but Bobby Ferillo's call-up this year has struck a particular chord with all of us."

He gestured toward the empty chair on the front row, a place reserved for Bobby's family. "Bobby isn't just a name on a list. He's not just another young man sent off to do his duty. He's a part of this town—a part of our story. His music brought life to our gatherings, his talent reminded us of what's possible, and his future symbolized the hope we all carried for our children."

The mayor paused, his gaze scanning the room, meeting the eyes of parents, siblings, and neighbors who shared his burden. "This was supposed to be the year things began to ease. The year we could start to imagine a world where our sons stayed here, building the lives they dreamed of instead of being sent away. Instead, the draft continues to take them from us, one by one."

A murmur of agreement rippled through the crowd, soft but poignant. Families exchanged glances, some filled with fear, others with quiet resignation. The atmosphere was thick with the understanding that while the war might seem far away, its consequences remained close—too close.

Mayor Richards placed both hands on the lectern, leaning forward slightly. "We may not be able to change this outcome, but we can choose how we respond. Bobby—and every boy from this town who has been called up—

needs to know they are not alone. That no matter how far they go, they carry this community with them. That we are here, thinking of them, praying for them, and waiting for the day they come home."

Angelica sat in the audience beside John, her hands folded tightly in her lap. "We have to do something," she whispered to him.

"There's not much we can do," John replied, his voice low. "The draft doesn't leave room for negotiation."

Angelica's gaze was fixed on the stage. "Then we remind Bobby and all of them that they're not alone. We send letters, care packages, anything to show them that we're thinking of them. They need to know that this town is behind them."

John nodded. "That, we can do."

The following week, Jane's School organized a letter-writing campaign. Students of all ages filled the music room, writing messages of support and encouragement for Bobby. Some drew pictures, others included prayers, and a few wrote heartfelt notes about how much Bobby's music had inspired them.

Angelica supervised the activity, her voice soft and encouraging as she moved from table to table. When she reached Andy, she paused.

He sat with his pencil hovering above the paper, his brow furrowed.

"Andy," Angelica said gently, kneeling beside him. "It's all right if you don't know what to say. Just write from your heart."

Andy looked at her, his eyes troubled. "What if he doesn't come back?"

The question hung heavy in the air. Angelica took a deep breath, placing a comforting hand on his arm. "We hope. We pray. And we keep believing in him, no matter what."

Andy nodded slowly, his pencil finally touching the paper.

The day Bobby left, the entire town seemed to gather at the bus stop. The mood was subdued, the usual chatter replaced by quiet handshakes and tearful hugs.

Angelica and John stood near the Ferillo family, their presence a steadying force.

"You'll come back to us, Bobby," Angelica said firmly, her hands clasping his. "Promise me."

"I promise, Miss Thompson," Bobby said, his voice thick with emotion.

John extended a hand, his grip strong. "Take care of yourself, Bobby. And don't forget—you've got an entire town waiting for you."

Bobby nodded, swallowing hard. "I won't forget."

As the bus pulled away, the crowd waved, their faces a mix of pride and grief. The war had claimed another of their own, and the waiting had begun.

Angelica stood beside John, her shoulders square but her heart heavy. "Do you think he'll be all right?"

John didn't answer immediately. His gaze lingered on the bus as it disappeared down the road. "I don't know," he said quietly. "But I do know that whatever happens, he'll carry this town with him. And we'll carry him in our hearts."

The wind rustled the leaves of the maples outside the school, their branches swaying as if to echo his words.

That evening, after the town had quieted and the last of the goodbyes had been whispered, John and Angelica returned home. The weight of the day hung heavy between them, unspoken but present.

Angelica moved through the house with a purposeful air, setting her purse on the table, pouring two cups of tea, and placing one in front of John where he sat at the kitchen table.

"You've been quiet," John said after a moment, his eyes following her as she took her seat across from him.

"I've been thinking," Angelica replied, wrapping her hands around the warm mug. "About Bobby. About all the boys this war has taken. And about how unfair it is."

John nodded, his face lined with worry. "It's cruel. They're barely old enough to understand the world, let alone fight in someone else's war."

She took a sip of her tea, her gaze fixed on the table. "Do you remember the first time Bobby played the piano for us? He was so nervous, his hands shaking like leaves. And now those same hands are being sent to hold a rifle."

Her voice wavered, and she set the cup down, staring at it as though it could hold answers to questions that had none.

John reached across the table, his hand covering hers. "You gave him more than music, Angelica. You gave him confidence, a way to see the world as something bigger and brighter than he ever thought it could be. He'll carry that with him, even in a place like Vietnam."

Angelica looked up, her green eyes filled with unshed tears. "What if it's not enough? What if—" She cut herself off, her throat tightening.

He stood and moved to her side, pulling her gently into his arms. She leaned into him, her head resting against his chest as her tears fell.

"It has to be enough," John said quietly, his voice steady. "It's all we can give him now. And he'll carry it. I know he will."

Later, they sat on the porch, the night air cool and still, the crickets a faint hum in the distance. Angelica wrapped a blanket around her shoulders, her gaze fixed on the stars.

"I can't stop thinking about his mother," she said softly. "How she held onto him so tightly at the bus stop. It was like she couldn't bear to let go."

John nodded, his expression pensive. "No parent should have to send their child off to war. It's a kind of heartbreak I can't imagine."

Angelica turned to him, her voice quieter now. "Do you think the town will ever feel the same? After all this?"

John took a moment to answer, his hand finding hers under the blanket. "I don't think anything ever stays the same, Angelica. But this town is strong. It's seen hard times before, and it's still standing. The people here—they're resilient. Just like you."

She smiled faintly, though the sadness lingered in her eyes. "I wish resilience didn't have to come at such a cost."

The wind picked up slightly, rustling the leaves of the trees around their house. Angelica pulled the blanket tighter around her.

"When this war is over," she said, her voice firm, "we have to find a way to make sure these boys—Bobby, all of them—know they're not forgotten. That their sacrifices meant something."

"We will," John promised, his voice quiet but resolute. "Whatever happens, we'll find a way to honor them."

Angelica leaned her head on his shoulder, the weight of the day finally easing under the steady rhythm of his breathing.

And as the stars flickered above, the echoes of the day lingered in the air—a reminder of the lives changed, the lives at risk, and the unshakable hope that still endured.

The Diagnosis That Changed Everything

1972

The waiting room of the doctor's office was quiet, save for the faint rustle of magazines being flipped and the hum of fluorescent lights overhead. Angelica sat with her hands folded tightly in her lap, her knuckles pale against her green dress. She stared straight ahead, but her focus was distant, as if she were trying to will herself somewhere else entirely.

Beside her, John sat stiffly, his hands gripping the arms of his chair. His usual calm composure was nowhere to be found. Instead, his jaw was tight, his eyes fixed on the door to the exam room. He'd never felt so powerless in his life.

When the nurse called Angelica's name, she rose quickly, brushing her dress as if preparing for a performance. John stood as well, his hand lightly touching her back as they followed the nurse into the sterile, brightly lit room.

Dr. Patel was already seated at his desk, his expression kind but serious. He gestured for them to sit.

"Angelica, John," he began, glancing between them. "Thank you for coming in. I know the waiting has been difficult."

Angelica nodded, her lips pressing into a thin line. John's grip on her hand tightened, and she squeezed back as if to steady him.

Dr. Patel folded his hands on the desk, his gaze soft but direct. "The results of your biopsy have come in. It's cancer."

The words landed like a thunderclap.

Angelica inhaled sharply, her free hand moving instinctively to her chest. John blinked, his mind struggling to process the doctor's words.

"What… what kind of cancer?" Angelica managed, her voice calm but trembling at the edges.

"Breast cancer," Dr. Patel said gently. "The good news is that we've caught it relatively early. But it's aggressive, and we'll need to act quickly."

John's voice finally broke through the thick silence. "What does that mean? What's the treatment? What are the chances?"

Dr. Patel nodded at the barrage of questions, his demeanor patient. "Treatment will likely involve surgery followed by chemotherapy. The prognosis is hopeful, but it depends on how the cancer responds to treatment."

Angelica nodded slowly, her mind visibly turning over the information. "And if I don't respond well?"

Dr. Patel's expression softened further. "We'll take it one step at a time. For now, our focus is on removing the tumor and beginning the necessary therapies. I'll be with you through every stage, Angelica."

She nodded again, her lips moving as if to say something, but no words came out.

The drive home was quiet. Rain streaked against the windshield, blurring the road ahead. Angelica stared out the passenger-side window, her breath fogging the glass slightly. John kept his hands firmly on the wheel, his knuckles white.

When they pulled into the driveway, Angelica didn't move immediately. She sat still, her gaze fixed on the drops sliding down the window.

"Angelica," John said softly, turning to her. "Talk to me."

She turned to him, her eyes brimming with unshed tears. "I'm scared, John."

The words shattered something inside him. He reached out, pulling her into his arms. "I know," he whispered, his voice breaking. "I am too."

They stayed like that for a long moment, the rain tapping against the roof like a heartbeat.

Later that evening, they sat together in the living room. Angelica had lit a fire in the hearth, the flickering flames casting warm light across the room. She sat on the couch, her legs tucked beneath her, while John paced near the mantel.

"We'll fight this," John said, his voice firm. "Whatever it takes, Angelica, we'll fight."

She looked up at him, her face soft but resolute. "I'm not giving up, John. But… I need you to know something."

He stopped pacing, turning to her. "What?"

"If the worst happens, I don't want you to carry this alone," she said, her voice steady despite the emotion behind it. "Promise me you'll let people help you. Promise me you'll keep going, for the school, for the children."

John sank onto the couch beside her, taking her hands in his. "Don't talk like that. You're not going anywhere. We'll get through this together."

"I know," she said, leaning her forehead against his. "But I need you to promise anyway."

He closed his eyes, his grip on her hands tightening. "I promise," he whispered.

Angelica smiled faintly, her fingers brushing his cheek. "Good. Because I'm not done yet, John Anderson. Not with you, not with the school, not with life."

He managed a small smile in return, his resolve hardening. "Neither am I."

As the fire crackled softly, they held each other, their love and determination filling the quiet room. The storm in their lives had just begun, but they were determined to face it together, come what may.

One Last Christmas at School

1973

The scent of pine and cinnamon filled the air, mingling with the cheerful hum of conversation and laughter. The gymnasium was transformed into a winter wonderland, with strings of twinkling lights casting a warm glow over the walls and garlands of holly draped across every surface. A tall Christmas tree stood in the corner, its branches heavy with handmade ornaments contributed by students and staff.

Angelica stood near the piano, her hands brushing over the keys as she played a soft, familiar carol. Her green dress shimmered faintly in the light, and though her frame was thinner than before, her smile was as radiant as ever.

"Miss Thompson! Play 'Jingle Bells' next!" a student called, his voice bright with excitement.

"Coming right up!" Angelica replied, her tone as cheerful as the child's. She glanced at John, who stood near the refreshment table, watching her with a mixture of pride and quiet sadness.

John walked over, a mug of cider in each hand. He handed one to her and leaned slightly against the piano. "You've still got it," he said softly, his voice carrying over the hum of the room.

Angelica took the mug, her fingers brushing his. "I'd better. Can't let the students down, especially tonight."

John glanced around the gymnasium. Students of all ages mingled with their families, teachers chatting in small groups near the refreshments, and Mrs. Whitman directing a group of sixth-graders as they set up chairs for the evening's carol sing-along.

"It's a good turnout," John said.

"It is," Angelica agreed, her gaze sweeping over the room. "The best part of this job, don't you think? Seeing everyone come together like this?"

John nodded, his throat tightening. He took a sip of his cider to cover his emotion.

As the evening progressed, the students took turns performing carols on stage. A group of fourth-graders sang *Silent Night,* their young voices sweet and tentative, while a trio of fifth-graders played *Deck the Halls* on recorders, earning laughter and applause from the crowd.

Finally, it was Angelica's turn. She stood and walked to the piano, her steps deliberate but graceful.

"This one's for everyone," she said, her voice warm. "But especially for my family here at Jane's School. Thank you all for making this such a special place."

Her fingers glided over the keys, and the first notes of *Have Yourself a Merry Little Christmas* filled the room. The crowd grew quiet, their attention fixed on

Angelica as her music wove through the space, wrapping everyone in its gentle embrace.

John watched from the edge of the room, his hands clasped in front of him. She was pouring everything into the song—her love for the school, her gratitude for the community, her determination to hold onto joy despite the weight of her diagnosis.

When the final note faded, the room erupted into applause. Angelica stood and gave a small bow, her smile lighting up the room.

Later, as the event wound down and the crowd began to thin, John and Angelica found themselves alone near the Christmas tree.

"Are you tired?" John asked, his voice gentle.

"A little," Angelica admitted, leaning against him. "But it's the good kind of tired."

John wrapped an arm around her shoulders, pulling her close. "You were incredible tonight."

She tilted her head to look up at him, her eyes sparkling. "We were incredible, John. This school—everything we've built here—it's ours. It's part of us."

He nodded, swallowing the lump in his throat. "It always will be."

Angelica reached out, plucking an ornament from the tree—a simple red star made of felt, stitched with a child's careful hand. "This place has given us so much. And tonight, it gave me something else."

"What's that?" John asked.

"Hope," she said softly, turning the star over in her hands. "Even with everything we're facing, I feel… at peace. Being here, with you, with them—it's enough."

John placed his hand over hers, holding the ornament together. "We'll get through this, Angelica. Together."

She smiled, leaning into him as the twinkling lights reflected in her eyes. "Together," she echoed.

As the last of the guests left and the gym fell silent, they stood by the tree, savoring the warmth of the moment. It was a Christmas they would never forget—a testament to their love, their resilience, and the community that had become their family.

Her Last Lesson

1974

The hospital room was quiet, the muffled sounds of nurses in the hallway barely audible through the closed door. Sunlight filtered through the blinds, casting soft stripes across the pale walls. The faint scent of antiseptic lingered in the air, but to John, it was the weight of time that pressed most heavily on the room.

Angelica lay in the narrow bed, her auburn hair now streaked with silver and thinner than it had once been. Her skin was pale but still warm as John held her hand in both of his. The steady beeping of the heart monitor was a quiet reminder that each moment was precious.

"John," she said softly, her voice thinner but carrying the same strength he had always known.

He leaned closer, his fingers tightening around hers. "I'm here, Angelica."

She smiled faintly, her green eyes meeting his. "I need you to listen to me."

"You don't have to say anything," he said quickly, his voice breaking. "Just rest."

Her smile grew, soft but knowing. "Stubborn as ever. But this isn't about me. It's about you—and the school."

John blinked back tears, his heart aching at the thought of losing her. "Angelica—"

"Let me finish," she said gently but firmly. "We've built something special, John. Together. The school, the children, the community—it's all part of us. But it can't stay frozen in time."

John shook his head slightly, his brow furrowing. "You don't need to worry about that right now. The school will be fine."

"Will it?" she asked, her tone probing. "You've always resisted change, John. But change is what keeps things alive. It's what keeps them growing. You have to embrace it. Promise me you will."

He swallowed hard, his chest tight. "Angelica, I—"

"Promise me," she said again, her voice trembling but resolute.

John bowed his head, his forehead brushing against her hand. "I promise."

She exhaled softly, her smile returning. "Good. That's all I needed to hear."

For a while, they sat in silence, the sun dipping lower in the sky. John thought back to their years together—the first time they met, the concerts they organized, the quiet moments in the music room.

"I don't know how to do this without you," he said finally, his voice barely above a whisper.

"You'll find a way," Angelica said, her eyes closing briefly before opening again. "You always do. And you're not alone. The school, the people there—they're your family, too."

He nodded, though the words didn't ease the ache in his chest.

"I'll always be with you, John," she murmured, her voice growing fainter. "In the music, in the laughter of the children, in the leaves falling outside the school. I'll be there."

Her grip on his hand weakened, and John's breath hitched. "Angelica…"

Her eyes opened one last time, her gaze steady. "Keep the school alive, John. Keep living."

And then she was gone, the faint smile on her lips a final gift.

The funeral was held a few days later in the small chapel where they had been married. The entire town seemed to turn out, filling the pews with a quiet, shared grief.

John stood near the altar, his shoulders heavy but his gaze steady as he spoke about Angelica's life and the impact she had left behind. He spoke of her passion, her generosity, and the way she had made everyone around her better.

"She believed in the power of change," he said, his voice steady despite the tears that threatened. "Not as something to fear, but as something to embrace. And she believed in all of us—our ability to carry on, to keep building, to keep growing."

When the service ended, the crowd lingered, sharing memories and quiet condolences.

That evening, John returned to the school. The halls were silent, the faint echo of his footsteps a reminder of all the years he and Angelica had walked them together.

He found himself in the music room, the piano standing like a sentinel in the soft light. Sitting on the bench, he reached out, his fingers brushing the keys. Slowly, he began to play one of Angelica's favorite melodies, the notes filling the empty space with warmth and sorrow.

As the final note faded, he looked out the window. The two great maples outside stood tall, their leaves swaying gently in the breeze. He could almost hear Angelica's voice, urging him forward.

And for the first time, he felt ready to try.

"I'll keep my promise," he whispered, his voice steady. "For you. For us."

The music room was quiet again, but the echoes of their shared purpose lingered, as enduring as the school itself.

In the days following Angelica's funeral, John moved through life as if in a fog. The world outside continued on as always—children played in the streets, neighbors mowed their lawns, the sun rose and set—but for John, time felt suspended. The warmth of Angelica's presence, her laughter, her steady hand in his life, was gone, and its absence was like an open wound.

At home, her favorite chair by the window sat empty, her books left in a neat stack on the side table. The house, once filled with music and light, now felt unbearably quiet.

John spent his evenings at the school. The familiar halls offered a kind of solace, though the emptiness pressed heavily on him. The music room became his refuge; he'd sit on the piano bench, staring at the keys, his hands resting uselessly in his lap.

One night, a knock at the door startled him. He turned to see Tom Ferillo, now a custodian at the school, standing hesitantly in the doorway.

"Mr. Anderson," Tom said, his voice low. "I saw the light on. Thought maybe you'd want some company."

John managed a faint smile and gestured for Tom to come in.

The two men sat in silence for a while, the unspoken weight of Angelica's absence filling the room. Finally, Tom spoke.

"She meant a lot to all of us," he said, his gaze fixed on the floor. "Especially to me and Bobby. She saw something in us, even when we didn't see it ourselves."

John nodded, his throat tightening. "She had a way of doing that. She believed in people, in their potential, even when they couldn't see it."

Tom hesitated before continuing. "You know, Bobby always said Miss Thompson was like a second mother to him. After he got drafted... she wrote to him every week. He said those letters kept him going."

The mention of Bobby—gone now for years, another casualty of the war—hit John like a punch to the chest. He looked away, his hands gripping the edge of the piano bench.

"She kept us all going," John said after a moment, his voice raw. "I don't know how to do this without her, Tom."

Tom looked at him, his eyes filled with quiet respect. "You don't have to do it alone, Mr. Anderson. You've got the school, the staff, the town. We're all here for you, the way you and Miss Thompson were always there for us."

John didn't respond right away, but he felt a flicker of something—gratitude, maybe, or hope—in Tom's words.

The next morning, John found himself standing beneath the two great maples outside the school. Their leaves, vibrant and green in the early summer sunlight, whispered softly in the breeze.

He remembered Angelica's voice, her unwavering belief in the power of change.

"You have to embrace it," she had said.

Taking a deep breath, John turned toward the building. The school stood resilient, a testament to everything he and Angelica had worked for.

In the days that followed, John threw himself into his work. He met with staff to discuss new programs, worked late into the evenings on budgets and proposals, and began planning a community event to honor Angelica's legacy. He didn't shy away from the changes she had urged him to accept; instead, he looked for ways to blend tradition with progress, ensuring the school remained a place of growth and connection.

Angelica's piano became a centerpiece of the music room. Students would often find John there, playing softly during his breaks. The melodies were a quiet reminder of her spirit, a way to keep her presence alive within the school.

One afternoon, as John stood in the music room watching a group of children rehearse for a recital, he felt a strange sense of peace. The laughter, the notes, the shared energy of the room—it all reminded him of Angelica.

She was gone, but she was still here, too. In the music, in the children's voices, in the very walls of the school they had built together.

That evening, as the sun set and the shadows of the maples stretched long across the playground, John sat at the piano. He placed his hands on the keys, playing the melody Angelica had taught him so many years ago.

As the last note faded, he whispered, "I'll keep living, Angelica. I'll keep the school alive. For you. For us."

The room fell silent, but the echoes of his promise lingered, as steadfast and enduring as the love that had shaped his life.

Tom the Janitor, Tom the Friend

1984

John stood near the glass doors at the front of the school, gazing out at the windswept leaves skittering across the walkway. The winter sun hung low, casting long shadows over the yard. He'd been lost in thought, the weight of the day heavy on his shoulders, when the sound of footsteps behind him broke the silence.

"Mr. Anderson?" a familiar voice called out, tentative but steady.

John turned to see Tom Ferillo standing a few feet away, a ring of keys dangling from his hand. His work shirt was faded but clean, with a patch reading "Tom" stitched over the left pocket. A faint smudge of grease streaked his cheek, and his dark hair was flecked with gray that hadn't been there the last time they'd spoken.

"Tom," John said, his voice softening with recognition.

"Didn't mean to sneak up on you," Tom said with a crooked smile, holding up the keys. "I've been making my rounds. Just got back from fixing the furnace."

John's lips curved into a faint smile. "So, you're the one keeping this place running now."

"Somebody's gotta do it," Tom said with a shrug, tucking the keys into his pocket. "Been back for a few months now. After Mom and Dad passed, it felt… right, coming back here. Familiar, you know?"

John nodded, his gaze shifting briefly to the hallway. "I've walked these halls more times than I can count, but today it feels different. Final."

Tom studied him for a moment, then leaned slightly against the wall. "I heard you were retiring."

"That's their plan," John said, though the words felt heavy in his mouth.

Tom nodded slowly, his eyes distant for a moment. "It's strange, isn't it? This place… it gets under your skin. No matter where I went or what I did, I always ended up thinking about these halls, the classrooms, the playground. Even when I wanted to leave it behind, it kept pulling me back."

John tilted his head slightly, his brow furrowing. "I thought you had left for good. I remember hearing you'd moved out west."

"I did," Tom said, his voice carrying a touch of weariness. "Tried my hand at a lot of things. Construction, truck driving, even a stint in sales. But none of it felt… solid. Like I didn't quite fit."

He paused, his gaze drifting to the lockers lining the hall. "When Bobby died, something shifted. I kept thinking about him, about all the times he'd sit in that music room with Miss Thompson, playing like he belonged to the world. It took me a lot of years to realize I wanted to be close to that, to what he loved, to come home."

John's throat tightened at the mention of Bobby, but he managed a small nod. "This school has always been more than just a building. It's a part of all of us."

"Yeah," Tom said, his smile faint but genuine. "That's why I came back. Started working odd jobs, helping out wherever I could. Before I knew it, I was here full-time, keeping the lights on and the floors clean. It's not much, but it feels... real."

John took a step closer, resting a hand on Tom's shoulder. "It's more than real, Tom. It's important. What you're doing here—keeping this place alive—it matters."

Tom looked down, his voice quiet. "You were always good at that, you know? Making people feel like they mattered."

John's smile deepened, though his eyes glistened. "I learned from the best. This school, these people—they taught me as much as I taught them."

For a moment, the two men stood in silence, the weight of shared history settling comfortably between them.

"You staying long today?" Tom asked, breaking the quiet.

"Just taking one last walk," John said, his tone reflective. "Trying to say goodbye, though I'm not sure I know how."

Tom nodded, a hint of understanding in his eyes. "Well, if you need anything, I'll be around. Got a couple of leaky faucets to fix before the day's out."

John chuckled softly. "Good to know the place is in capable hands."

As Tom turned to leave, he paused and glanced back over his shoulder. "You know, Mr. Anderson, this school's not really losing you. Not really. You've left too much of yourself here for that."

John's chest tightened, but he managed a small nod. "Thank you, Tom. That means a lot."

Tom gave a faint smile before heading down the hallway, his footsteps fading into the quiet.

John watched him go, his heart heavier but steadier. Tom's presence—his return to the school and his quiet dedication—was proof that the spirit of Jane's School would endure, carried by those who understood its true value.

Turning back toward the glass doors, John took a deep breath, ready to continue his walk through the echoes of his past.

A Note Left Unplayed

The late afternoon sun filtered through the tall windows, casting soft, golden light onto the worn tile floor. Dust motes floated lazily in the air, illuminated by the slanting rays. John Anderson walked slowly, his footsteps quiet but deliberate, the familiar creak of the floor beneath him stirring memories he had tucked away for years.

When he reached the music room, he stopped. The door was ajar, the room beyond cloaked in shadows. His breath caught in his throat as he gently pushed the door open.

The room was as he remembered it, though time had softened its edges. The piano sat in the same place, its black surface dulled by a thin layer of dust. The rows of chairs were neatly arranged, waiting for students who would never come. On the far wall, a bulletin board displayed faded flyers from long-past concerts, their colors muted but their significance undiminished.

John stepped inside, his gaze sweeping the space. It felt smaller than it once had, though the memories it held loomed large.

He moved to the piano, his hand brushing over the keys. A soft, discordant note sounded, startling him. He chuckled faintly, shaking his head. "Still needs tuning," he murmured.

The piano had been Angelica's heart, the place where her passion and joy radiated most clearly. He could almost see her sitting there, her auburn hair catching the light as she played, her fingers coaxing melodies from the keys that seemed to bring the entire school to life.

John sat on the bench, the wood creaking slightly under his weight. His fingers hovered over the keys, trembling. Slowly, he played a few notes of *Have Yourself a Merry Little Christmas.* It was the song Angelica had played at their last Christmas concert together, her voice filling the gymnasium, weaving warmth and hope into every corner of the room.

The notes faltered, his hands lowering to his lap as his emotions swelled.

"You'd hate to see it so quiet, wouldn't you?" he said softly, his voice breaking the stillness.

He could almost hear her reply, teasing but kind. *It's not the quiet that matters, John. It's what you fill it with.*

His gaze drifted to the bulletin board. Among the faded flyers and tattered sheet music was a photo of Angelica at the piano, surrounded by students. The image was worn, but her smile shone through, undimmed by time.

"You were the soul of this place," John whispered, his voice thick. "You gave these kids something I never could. You gave them music, joy... hope."

He leaned forward, his elbows on his knees, his hands clasped tightly together. "I've tried, Angelica. I've tried to keep it alive, to honor what we built. But it feels... harder now. Without you."

The quiet of the room seemed to answer him, the faint echoes of years past filling the space.

After a long moment, John stood, his movements slow but deliberate. He placed a hand on the piano, his touch lingering.

"I promised you I'd keep the school alive," he said, his voice steady despite the emotion in his eyes. "And I will. No matter what, I'll find a way."

He turned to leave, pausing at the doorway to take one last look. The light had shifted, casting the room in a soft, warm glow. For a moment, he could almost believe she was still there, her presence as vibrant as ever.

With a deep breath, he stepped into the hallway, the echoes of Angelica's music following him, a quiet reminder of everything they had shared—and everything he still had to carry forward.

The New Year's Return

1985

The first day back after Winter Break always carried a buzz of energy. The crisp January air bit at the cheeks of students as they filed off buses, their laughter and chatter cutting through the quiet morning. Teachers, bundled in heavy coats and scarves, greeted one another with warm smiles and updates on their holidays.

John Anderson stood by the main entrance, his posture straight despite the slight ache in his knees. His overcoat hung neatly on his shoulders, and his hands were clasped behind his back as he watched the scene unfold. For decades, he'd performed this same ritual, welcoming the school's return to life after its brief hibernation.

But this year was different. This was the beginning of his last semester as principal.

"Good morning, Mr. Anderson!" a student called out, her face framed by a bright red scarf.

"Morning, Lydia," John replied, his smile crinkling the corners of his eyes. "How was your break?"

"Too short!" she said with a grin, her boots crunching on the salted pavement as she hurried inside.

John chuckled softly, shaking his head. Children were always so eager to escape school until they had to be away from it.

Behind him, the familiar voice of Tom Ferillo called out. "You're going to catch frostbite standing there, Mr. Anderson."

John turned to see Tom holding a salt bucket in one hand and a mop handle in the other. His work boots left damp prints on the tiles as he stepped inside, shaking snow from his jacket.

"It's tradition," John replied, his tone warm. "The kids expect to see me here."

Tom set the bucket down, his breath fogging the air as he spoke. "If they knew you'd been out here freezing for half an hour, they'd tell you to head inside."

John smiled. "I'll go in when the buses are empty."

Tom tilted his head, a faint grin on his face. "Stubborn as ever. I'll get you some coffee to thaw out when you're done."

John nodded his thanks, watching as Tom disappeared down the hall, his steady presence a quiet reassurance.

By mid-morning, the school hummed with activity. Children filled the hallways, their voices a joyful cacophony. Teachers returned to their classrooms, tidying desks and setting up lesson plans.

John made his rounds, stopping briefly in each room to greet the staff and students. In the second-grade classroom, Mrs. Whitman was leading a cheerful discussion about New Year's resolutions. In the art room, Ms. Perez was setting up paints for a winter-themed project.

When he reached the music room, he paused in the doorway. The piano stood gleaming in the sunlight that streamed through the windows, its presence a reminder of Angelica.

Ms. Carter, the young music teacher who had just taken over the program, looked up and smiled. "Good morning, Mr. Anderson."

"Good morning," John said, stepping inside. His eyes drifted to the walls, now adorned with posters of famous composers and drawings by students. "The room looks wonderful, Ms. Carter. You've made it your own."

She beamed. "Thank you. But a lot of the credit belongs to the kids. They've got so much enthusiasm—it makes my job easy."

John nodded, his chest tightening with a bittersweet mix of pride and longing. "Angelica would be proud."

Later, as lunchtime approached, John stood in the main hall, greeting students as they passed by. A group of sixth graders approached, their laughter infectious.

"Mr. Anderson, are you coming to the science fair next week?" one of them asked.

"I wouldn't miss it," John replied. "Just make sure your projects are ready. I hear the competition is stiff this year."

The students grinned and hurried off, their excitement clear.

By the time the final bell rang, the school had settled into its familiar rhythm. John returned to his office, sitting at the desk that had been his for so many years. The sound of children's voices echoed faintly in the distance, a comforting reminder of why he had devoted his life to this place.

A knock at the door pulled him from his thoughts.

"Come in," John called.

Tom stepped inside, a thermos of coffee in his hand. "Figured you could use this," he said, placing it on the desk.

John smiled, leaning back in his chair. "Thanks, Tom. You're keeping me going these days."

Tom shrugged, his grin modest. "Just returning the favor. You've kept this place running for a lot longer than I have."

John looked out the window, his gaze thoughtful. "It's strange to think this is my last first day back. After all these years, I don't know how to say goodbye to it."

Tom's voice was quiet but steady. "You don't have to say goodbye, Mr. Anderson. You've built too much here. It's going to keep going, because of you."

John nodded slowly, his eyes glistening. "That means more than you know, Tom."

As Tom left, John leaned back in his chair, the thermos warm in his hands. Outside, the snow began to fall again, blanketing the school in a soft, quiet stillness.

The new year had begun, and with it, the final chapter of John's journey at Jane's School. But as he watched the snow settle over the playground, he felt a quiet reassurance that the legacy he and Angelica had built would endure, carried forward by those who understood its worth.

Bobby's Song

The janitor's closet was a small, cluttered space tucked away near the gymnasium, filled with the scent of cleaning supplies and the faint metallic tang of old tools. Tom Ferillo sat on an upturned crate, a mop leaning against the wall beside him. In his hands was an old, dog-eared photograph—a black-and-white image of Bobby at the piano, his face lit with concentration as his fingers danced over the keys.

The faint hum of a vacuum cleaner echoed down the hall, but Tom didn't notice. His thoughts were elsewhere, his eyes locked on the photo.

"I used to think you'd be famous," he said softly, his voice breaking the quiet. "World-class pianist. That's what they always said."

The words hung in the air, and Tom let out a shaky breath.

A knock at the door startled him. He quickly slid the photograph into his pocket as John Anderson peeked inside.

"Am I interrupting?" John asked, his tone gentle.

Tom shook his head. "No, just taking a quick break."

John stepped inside, glancing around the cramped room before leaning against the doorframe. "You've been at it all day. Thought you might want some company."

Tom nodded, his fingers fidgeting with the edge of his work shirt. "Yeah. That'd be nice."

John looked at him, his gaze searching. "You've been quiet today. Something on your mind?"

Tom hesitated, then pulled the photograph from his pocket and handed it to John. "Found this in one of the old lockers last week. Brought back a lot of memories."

John studied the photo, his expression softening. "Bobby at the piano," he murmured. "Angelica used to say he played like the music was part of him."

Tom smiled faintly. "She was right. He was... different. Special."

Tom leaned forward, resting his elbows on his knees. "You know, when we were kids, I used to be jealous of him. Everyone loved Bobby. The teachers, the kids, even Mom and Dad. He was the golden boy."

John handed the photo back, his voice measured. "You felt like you were living in his shadow."

"Yeah," Tom admitted. "But it wasn't just that. He was so good at everything. Music, school... even just talking to people. It was like he belonged wherever he went."

Tom's voice grew quieter. "And then he was gone. Just like that. One letter, one draft notice, and then Vietnam took him."

John nodded solemnly. "He was a bright light, Tom. Losing him dimmed this town in ways we're still feeling."

Tom rubbed his hands together, his voice heavy with regret. "I used to wonder what he'd think of me now. Fixing leaky pipes and sweeping floors. He'd probably laugh. Say something like, 'Tom, you were always meant for more.'"

John straightened, his tone firm. "He wouldn't laugh. And you are more, Tom. What you do here—it matters. You've kept this place going when it could've fallen apart. That's a legacy Bobby would be proud of."

Tom looked up, his eyes glistening. "You really think so?"

"I know so," John said, his voice unwavering. "Bobby's talent inspired people, but so does your dedication. You're just as much a part of this school as he was."

For a moment, the two men sat in silence, the weight of shared memories filling the space.

Tom finally stood, slipping the photograph back into his pocket. "You know, I don't think a day goes by when I don't think about him. What he could've done, who he could've been. But maybe... maybe I can carry some of that for him. Keep his memory alive."

John placed a hand on Tom's shoulder, his grip steady. "You already are, Tom. And as long as this school stands, so will his legacy—and yours."

Tom nodded, a small smile breaking through his grief. "Thanks, Mr. Anderson."

John smiled back. "Anytime."

As John left the room, Tom turned back to the photo one last time, his heart lighter than it had been in years. Bobby's legacy wasn't just in the music he had played or the dreams he had carried—it was in the people he had touched, and in the brother who still honored him every day.

Spring's Whisper

The cemetery was quiet, the kind of stillness that only spring mornings seemed to hold. A light breeze carried the scent of freshly cut grass and blooming daffodils, their yellow petals dotting the landscape like small bursts of sunlight.

John Anderson walked slowly along the gravel path, his hands clasped behind his back. He had passed these same rows of headstones countless times, but his steps always slowed when he neared hers.

The simple stone stood beneath a maple tree just beginning to sprout its leaves. Her name—*Angelica Thompson Anderson*—was etched cleanly into the granite, along with the years of her too-short life and the words she had chosen herself:

"In every note, a life lived."

John stopped a few feet away, his breath hitching slightly as he took in the sight. He rarely came here. Not because he didn't want to, but because it was still too raw, even years later.

He removed his hat, brushing a hand through his silver hair before stepping closer.

"Hello, Angelica," he said softly, his voice catching in the breeze. He bent slightly, brushing away a few stray leaves that had settled against the base of the stone.

"I know it's been a while," he admitted, his tone apologetic. "Longer than it should have been. But you probably guessed why I'm here."

He sighed, straightening and staring at the tree above him. Its branches swayed gently, the fresh green buds trembling in the breeze.

"They're trying to force me out," he said, his voice firmer now. "The board's been after me for months. They say it's time for new leadership, time for 'progress.' But I know what they're really planning."

His jaw tightened, and he looked back down at the headstone. "They want to close the school, Angelica. They think they can just padlock the doors and walk away, like it's some old building no one needs anymore. Like it isn't the heart of this town."

He paused, his hands gripping the brim of his hat tightly. "I can't let them do it. I won't. As long as I'm there, as long as I'm principal, they can't shut it down. And if they think I'm going to go quietly into retirement, they've got another thing coming."

The breeze picked up slightly, rustling the branches above. A single daffodil, its stem bent, leaned precariously at the edge of the grave. John knelt, carefully righting it and pressing the soil gently around its base.

"I know what you'd say," he murmured. "You'd tell me to think of the children. To put their future ahead of my pride. But it's not pride, Angelica.

It's about what we built. What this school stands for. If they close it, they're not just shutting down a building—they're erasing a legacy. Your legacy."

His voice cracked, and he bowed his head. "And mine too, I suppose."

For a long moment, he stayed there, the silence of the cemetery wrapping around him like a shroud.

When he finally stood, his knees aching slightly from the effort, his expression was resolute.

"I'll fight for it, Angelica," he said, his voice low but steady. "Not because I'm afraid of change, but because some things are worth holding onto. Some things deserve to be protected."

He placed his hat back on his head and stepped back, his gaze lingering on the stone.

"I wish you were here," he said softly. "You always knew how to make me see things more clearly. I'll try to remember what you'd do—what you'd want me to do. And I'll keep fighting until the last bell rings."

The breeze swirled gently around him, lifting a strand of his silver hair as if in reply.

John took a deep breath, letting the scent of spring fill his lungs. Then he turned and walked back down the path, his steps steadier now, his mind made up.

The fight wasn't over yet. And as long as he had breath in his body, he wasn't going to let Jane's School fade into memory.

The First Drops of Rain

The sky over Jane's School had darkened throughout the afternoon, a deep slate gray stretching from horizon to horizon. The sharp, clean air that preceded a storm swept through the town, rustling the brittle leaves that still clung to the two great maples by the school's entrance.

John Anderson stood near the front doors, his coat buttoned tightly against the growing chill. The wind tugged at his scarf, sending it flapping behind him as he squinted at the horizon. The first faint rumble of thunder rolled in the distance, low and ominous.

"It's going to be a strong one," Tom Ferillo said as he joined John, his hands tucked into his jacket pockets.

John nodded, his eyes never leaving the darkening sky. "The kind that leaves its mark."

Tom glanced around the empty schoolyard, the playground equipment swaying slightly in the rising wind. "You think the place will hold up? With everything going on, I'd hate to see it take more damage now."

John's jaw tightened. "This school has seen worse. It'll hold."

The first drops of rain splattered against the windows, leaving streaks that caught the faint light from the streetlamps. Inside, the school's halls were eerily quiet, their usual echoes replaced by the sound of the wind battering the walls.

Tom adjusted his cap, pulling it lower over his forehead. "I should check the boiler room. Make sure we don't have any leaks down there."

John gave a faint nod. "Go on, then. I'll lock up the last of the classrooms."

As Tom headed down the hallway, his footsteps fading into the distance, John lingered by the music room. The door stood slightly ajar, and he pushed it open, stepping inside.

The room was dim, the fading light from the storm barely illuminating the piano in the corner. The wind howled outside, rattling the windows and sending shivers through the old panes.

John moved to the piano, running his fingers lightly over its worn surface. He could still hear the echoes of Angelica's melodies in his mind, the way her music had filled this room and spilled out into the hall, lifting the spirits of anyone who heard it.

The wind slammed against the building with a forceful gust, shaking the walls and snapping John out of his reverie.

By the time he returned to the front entrance, the rain had intensified, pelting the windows in relentless sheets. The wind roared, bending the branches of the maples and sending loose leaves swirling through the air like a chaotic dance.

Tom emerged from the hallway, his coat damp from his trek to the boiler room. "No leaks so far," he reported, though his expression was grim. "But this storm's just getting started."

John nodded, his gaze fixed on the storm raging outside. "It feels... different. Like it's not just a storm."

Tom tilted his head. "What do you mean?"

John didn't answer immediately. Instead, he rested his hand on the doorframe, his fingers brushing the cold metal. "It feels like a turning point," he said finally. "Like it's trying to tell us something."

Tom frowned but didn't press further. Instead, he adjusted his jacket and stepped closer to the window. "Let's just hope it's not telling us to pack up and run."

John chuckled softly, though there was little humor in it. "This school's been here for over seventy years. It's not going anywhere without a fight."

As the two men stood side by side, the storm continued to grow. Lightning streaked across the sky, illuminating the flagpole and the shadowed playground for a brief, stark moment before plunging everything back into darkness.

The storm was here, and John could feel its power pressing against the walls, testing the resilience of the place he had called home for so long.

"It's going to be a long night," he said quietly.

Tom nodded. "We'll get through it. We always do."

But as the wind howled and the rain lashed against the glass, John couldn't shake the feeling that this storm carried more than just weather—it carried the weight of change, inevitable and unrelenting.

A Visit and A Reminder

The house felt larger during spring break, its corners echoing with the kind of silence that only Angelica's absence could create. John Anderson sat in his armchair by the front window, a cup of coffee cooling in his hands. Outside, the yard was bursting with life—daffodils in bloom, the maple trees stretching their budding branches toward the bright sky.

But the liveliness of the season didn't quite reach him. Not today.

The knock at the door startled him from his reverie. Setting his cup down, he stood, stretching his stiff joints before making his way to the entryway.

When he opened the door, Clara stood there, her warm smile framed by strands of gray hair escaping her neatly tied bun. Behind her were James and Nichole, both laden with overnight bags and looking slightly awkward.

"Hello, John," Clara said, stepping forward to give him a quick hug. "Hope we're not catching you at a bad time."

"Clara," John replied, his tone softening as he returned the hug. "It's good to see you. And you two—" he nodded at James and Nichole, "—welcome back. Been a long time."

"Too long," James said, his smile polite but unsure.

Nichole offered a small wave. "Thanks for having us, Uncle John."

Uncle. The word settled in John's chest like a bittersweet echo. "Come on in," he said, stepping aside. "Don't just stand there like you're on the porch of a stranger."

The house soon buzzed with a kind of energy John hadn't realized he'd been missing. Clara commandeered the kitchen, filling the air with the warm aroma of coffee and cookies. James brought in firewood for the small hearth in the living room, and Nichole set the dining table without being asked.

But as John watched them from the doorway, he couldn't shake the feeling that they'd rather be somewhere else.

"Sunny Florida," he muttered under his breath, shaking his head as he stepped back into the hallway. "That's where they ought to be. Not here with an old man like me."

The thought stayed with him throughout the afternoon. Over lunch, as they talked about James's new engineering job and Nichole's graduate studies in education, John couldn't help but feel like a relic, a reminder of the past they'd grown beyond.

"You're awfully quiet, John," Clara said, her tone light but probing as she set down her coffee cup.

"Just taking it all in," he replied, though his smile didn't quite reach his eyes.

Nichole tilted her head, studying him. "You're always like this when we visit."

"Like what?" he asked, raising an eyebrow.

"Like you don't think we want to be here," she said, her voice gentle but direct.

James chuckled softly. "She's right, you know. Every time we come back, you look like you're waiting for us to bolt for the door."

John opened his mouth to protest but stopped. They weren't wrong.

Later that evening, after James and Nichole had gone upstairs and Clara was busy washing dishes, John sat alone in the living room. The fire crackled softly in the hearth, the shadows flickering against the walls.

He leaned back in his chair, his thoughts wandering as they often did.

"Angelica," he murmured aloud, his voice low.

It wasn't unusual for him to talk to her in the quiet moments. He could almost hear her voice in reply, warm and steady, setting his perspective straight.

"They're here because they want to be," he imagined her saying, her tone full of affection but laced with that no-nonsense edge she reserved for him.

"They're young," he countered in his mind. "They've got their own lives, their own plans. They don't need to spend their time here."

"They don't *need* to," her voice responded in his memory, "but they're here anyway. Doesn't that tell you something?"

John exhaled, the corners of his mouth twitching into a faint smile. She was right, of course. She always was.

The next morning, as the spring sun poured through the windows, John found James in the backyard, helping Clara hang laundry on the line.

"Morning," John said, stepping onto the porch.

"Morning, Uncle John," James replied, glancing up.

John hesitated for a moment before walking over. "I was thinking... the old shed could use some fixing up. If you've got the time."

James grinned. "I'd like that."

They spent the better part of the morning working side by side, replacing rotted planks and hammering nails. As they worked, James shared stories about his job and his plans to design a new kind of bridge that could withstand harsher climates.

"That's impressive," John said, his tone sincere. "Angelica would've been proud of you."

James paused, his hammer in mid-air. "You think so?"

"I know so," John replied, his voice steady.

Meanwhile, inside the house, Nichole and Clara were organizing old photo albums.

"This one," Nichole said, holding up a picture of Angelica at the piano, "is my favorite."

Clara smiled softly. "She loved that piano more than anything. Except maybe John."

Nichole nodded, her voice quieter now. "I think Uncle John misses her more than he lets on."

Clara reached over, squeezing her daughter's hand. "He does. But having you two here—it means more to him than he'll ever say."

That night, after dinner, the four of them sat together by the fire. Nichole persuaded John to pull out Angelica's favorite record, and as the soft strains of a piano filled the room, she smiled.

"This reminds me of her," she said, her voice wistful.

"It reminds me of all of you," John replied, his gaze moving from James to Nichole to Clara. "Of the way Angelica always brought people together."

"She still does," Clara said softly, her eyes meeting his.

And in that moment, as the fire crackled and the music played, John felt the weight of his loneliness ease just a little.

Maybe Angelica had been right. They were here because they wanted to be, because they loved him. And maybe it was time he started letting them in.

For now, he would hold onto this moment—this spring, this family, this love—and trust in what Angelica had always known: some things were enduring, even in the quietest of lives.

The Fight for Jane's School

The morning air carried the unmistakable freshness of spring, mingled with the sound of children's laughter as they spilled out of buses and onto the schoolyard. Jane's School seemed to come alive after the break, its halls and playground echoing with the joy of return.

John Anderson stood near the front doors, his hands clasped behind his back as he greeted each child by name. His voice was warm, his posture as steady as the old flagpole outside, though his thoughts were elsewhere.

"Morning, Mr. Anderson!" a group of fourth graders called out, waving enthusiastically.

"Morning, morning!" John replied, tipping his hat slightly. "Don't forget— we've got field day coming up soon. Better start practicing those sack races!"

The children laughed, hurrying inside with renewed energy.

Behind him, a voice cut through the chatter.

"Principal Anderson?"

John turned to see a young woman striding purposefully up the walkway. Emily Carter, the district's newest official, was impeccably dressed in a tailored suit, her clipboard clutched tightly under one arm. Her heels clicked sharply against the pavement as she approached.

"Miss Carter," John said evenly, his tone polite but guarded.

"Good morning," she said, her smile tight and professional. "I'm here to speak with you. It's urgent."

John glanced at the buses still pulling in, the children streaming into the building, and then back at Emily.

"I'm sure it is," he said, his voice calm. "But I'm busy at the moment. First things first."

Her brow furrowed slightly, as though she hadn't anticipated resistance. "Mr. Anderson, this really can't wait—"

"Sure it can," John interrupted, gesturing toward the front doors. "My office is down the hall to the left. Make yourself comfortable. I'll be there when I'm done."

Emily opened her mouth to protest but closed it again, clearly realizing she wasn't going to win this battle. With a clipped nod, she turned and disappeared into the building, her heels echoing against the tiled floor.

John turned back to the schoolyard, his expression softening as he waved at the last group of children hopping off the bus.

"Morning, Mr. Anderson!"

"Morning, Danny," he called back, his voice warm. "Don't forget—spelling test tomorrow!"

The boy groaned theatrically, and John chuckled.

When the final bus rumbled away and the schoolyard cleared, John adjusted his hat and headed inside. He moved deliberately, each step measured. He knew what this meeting was about, and he wasn't going to let it rattle him.

When John entered his office, Emily was already seated, her clipboard resting on the desk. She looked up as he walked in, her expression composed but serious.

"Thank you for making time," she began, though her tone suggested she wasn't feeling particularly thankful.

John removed his hat, setting it on the coatrack before lowering himself into the chair behind his desk. "What can I do for you, Miss Carter?"

She straightened, her posture crisp. "Mr. Anderson, as you know, the district has been reviewing its resources and the allocation of funds across schools. After much deliberation, the board has decided—"

"To close Jane's School," John finished for her, his voice quiet but firm.

Emily hesitated, clearly caught off guard by his bluntness. "Yes," she said after a moment. "The decision was not made lightly, I assure you. But the new facility in the next town has more space, more modern amenities, and greater opportunities for the students. Consolidating resources will allow us to better serve the community as a whole."

John leaned back in his chair, his gaze steady. "Is that so?"

"Yes," Emily replied, her voice gaining confidence. "The students from Jane's will be bused to the new facility starting this fall. We're committed to ensuring a smooth transition for everyone involved."

John folded his hands on the desk, his expression unreadable. "And what about this community, Miss Carter? What happens to the families who rely on this school being right here, in their town?"

Emily's brow furrowed slightly. "Mr. Anderson, I understand this is difficult, but we have to look at the bigger picture—"

"No," John interrupted, his tone sharp enough to cut through her practiced speech. "The bigger picture is these children. These families. This isn't just a school to them, or to me. It's a home. It's a cornerstone of this town."

He stood, pacing slowly around the desk. "You and the board can sit in your shiny new office and talk about efficiency and progress all you like, but what you're doing isn't progress. It's erasure. You're taking something that's been the heart of this community for generations and tearing it out."

Emily shifted in her seat, clearly uncomfortable under his scrutiny. "Mr. Anderson, I respect your passion, but this decision has already been finalized. The closure is happening."

John stopped, turning to face her directly. "Not while I'm still breathing, it isn't."

The words hung in the air, heavy with defiance.

Emily stood, gathering her clipboard and smoothing her jacket. "I'll let the board know your feelings on the matter, but I'm afraid it won't change the outcome."

John's expression didn't waver. "You do that, Miss Carter. But let me make something clear—I'm not stepping down, and I'm not stepping aside. This school isn't closing without a fight."

She opened her mouth to reply but thought better of it, nodding curtly instead. Without another word, she turned and left the office, her heels clicking down the hall.

John sat back down, the quiet of the room settling around him. His eyes drifted to the picture on his desk—a photograph of him and Angelica, taken during one of their first fundraisers. Her smile was bright, her hand resting on his arm as they stood in front of the school's music room.

"I promised you," he murmured, his voice low but steady. "I promised I'd keep it alive."

Outside, the sound of children's laughter filtered through the open window, a reminder of everything he was fighting for.

The board might think the decision was final, but they didn't know John Anderson. And they didn't know Jane's School. Not the way he did.

This wasn't over. Not by a long shot.

Tom's Shadow Returns

The faint hum of the school's heating system filled the otherwise quiet janitor's closet. Tom Ferillo sat on an overturned bucket, his hands clasped together, elbows resting on his knees. Across from him, John Anderson perched on a stool, his cane leaning against the wall beside him.

Tom's usual easy demeanor was gone, replaced by a heaviness in his expression that John hadn't seen in years.

"You wanted to talk," John prompted gently, breaking the silence.

Tom nodded but didn't lift his gaze from the floor. "Yeah. I just... didn't know how to start."

John waited patiently, his years of teaching having taught him that silence often drew out what words couldn't.

Finally, Tom exhaled deeply and looked up. "It's about Bobby," he said, his voice low but steady. "And I know we talked about this, but you're the only one who really understands."

"It's natural, Tom," John said carefully, leaning forward. "You're human. Moving forward isn't easy. Sometimes we get stuck..."

Tom nodded absently, his fingers tightening around each other. "I just can't stop thinking about how much he could've done. All that talent, all that heart... and he never even got the chance."

John's brow furrowed slightly, but he nodded for Tom to continue.

"I've tried," Tom said, his voice cracking slightly. "I've tried to put it behind me, to focus on what's in front of me. But every time I walk into this school, I see him. Sitting in the music room, laughing with Miss Thompson. Or on the playground, showing off that stupid card trick he loved so much." He shook his head, his jaw tight. "And I can't help but think—why him? Why not me?"

John's heart ached at the rawness in Tom's voice. He shifted on the stool, his hand reaching out to rest on Tom's shoulder.

"Tom," he said firmly, "Bobby wouldn't want you to carry this weight forever. He'd want you to live your life, to find your own path—not to get stuck in the shadow of what might've been."

"I know that," Tom said, his eyes glistening. "I really do. But knowing it doesn't make it easier. I keep thinking... if I'd been more like him, maybe I could've—"

John cut him off, his tone gentle but resolute. "You're not Bobby, Tom. And you don't have to be. You've got your own gifts, your own way of making a difference. Look at what you're doing here. You're keeping this school alive, helping the kids who walk these halls now. That matters."

Tom looked away, his shoulders slumping slightly. "I don't feel like it's enough sometimes."

"It is," John said simply. "Because it's you. Bobby had his way of making the world better, and you've got yours. Don't compare them—just honor them both."

The room fell quiet again, the hum of the heating system filling the space.

Finally, Tom nodded slowly, his hand scrubbing over his face. "Thanks, Mr. Anderson. I needed to hear that."

John smiled faintly. "Anytime, Tom. That's what I'm here for."

Tom stood, his movements still heavy but with a touch more resolve. "Guess I should get back to work. Those lockers won't fix themselves."

John chuckled softly. "And I've got plenty to do myself."

As Tom opened the door, letting in the distant sound of children laughing in the hall, he paused and turned back.

"You know, Bobby always said you were the one who kept us all grounded. I think he was right."

John's smile softened, his voice quiet. "He kept us grounded, too, Tom. More than he ever knew."

With that, Tom left, and John sat alone in the quiet room, the weight of memory and legacy pressing gently but firmly against his thoughts.

A Calls to Arms

John sat at his desk, staring at the phone for a long moment. The echoes of Emily Carter's heels still lingered in his mind, a sharp and grating reminder of how swiftly they intended to dismantle everything.

He reached for the handset, his hand trembling slightly before he steadied it. Angelica's picture on the desk caught his eye, her vibrant smile frozen in time.

"I don't have your finesse," he muttered, his voice low. "But I'll try. For you. For them."

The first call was to the PTA president, a no-nonsense woman named Grace who had organized more bake sales and fundraisers than John could count. She listened quietly as he explained the situation, her silence unnerving.

"John," she said finally, her voice firm, "this is... this is terrible. But you know how these things go. The board doesn't backtrack once they've made up their minds."

"I know that," John replied, his tone sharp with frustration. "But they don't know this community like we do. If we can rally enough support, show them what this school means, maybe—"

"Maybe isn't much to go on," Grace interrupted, though her voice softened. "But I'll help. I'll start making calls to the parents. If we're going to do this, we need to act fast."

John exhaled, the tension in his chest easing slightly. "Thank you, Grace."

"Don't thank me yet," she said. "This is a long shot, and you know it."

The next call was to the mayor's office.

"John," Mayor Richards said, his tone hesitant, "I understand your position, but this is a district-level decision. My hands are tied."

"They're not tied," John shot back. "You just don't want to untie them."

The mayor sighed heavily. "You're asking me to go against the district. That's political suicide."

"I'm asking you to stand up for this town," John countered. "For the families who voted for you, who trust you to look out for them."

Richards hesitated, the line quiet for a moment. "I'll see what I can do," he said finally. "But don't hold your breath."

By the time John hung up the phone that evening, his throat was dry and his nerves frayed. The response was the same, call after call—support tempered by hesitation, help offered with conditions, and a steady undercurrent of defeat.

He sat back in his chair, rubbing his temples. The house was quiet, the only sound the faint ticking of the clock on the wall.

"This isn't enough," he muttered. "Not nearly enough."

The chair creaked as he leaned forward, his elbows on the desk. His mind churned, trying to piece together a plan that felt increasingly impossible.

"You'd know what to do," he said softly, looking at Angelica's picture. "You'd have them marching in the streets by now, wouldn't you?"

Her imagined response came easily, as it always did in his mind: *"Maybe. But you're the one they'll listen to, John. You've been their steady hand for years. They'll follow you."*

He shook his head, a wry smile tugging at his lips. "You always were better at making me believe in myself."

The next morning, John stood in the school gymnasium, looking out over a small but determined gathering. Parents, teachers, and a handful of local business owners filled the folding chairs, their faces a mix of worry and resolve.

Grace stood beside him, clipboard in hand. "It's not the whole town," she said quietly. "But it's a start."

John nodded, stepping forward to address the group.

"You all know why we're here," he began, his voice steady despite the weight in his chest. "The district wants to close Jane's School. They think it's just a building, that they can replace it with something newer, shinier, in the next town over. But we know better."

He paused, his eyes scanning the crowd. "This school isn't just a place. It's a part of this community. It's where we teach our children not just how to read and write, but how to care for one another. It's where we gather, where we grow. And I'm not going to let them take that away from us without a fight."

The room erupted into applause, though John noted the hesitation in some faces.

"We've got work to do," he continued, raising his voice over the clapping. "Letters to the board, petitions, rallies—whatever it takes to make them listen. I can't promise we'll win, but I can promise this: I'm not going to back down. And I hope none of you will, either."

Over the next few days, the school became a hub of activity. Parents signed petitions, students drew posters, and teachers wrote heartfelt letters to the district.

But as the days passed, the cracks in their effort began to show.

"John," Grace said one evening, pulling him aside in the staff room. "We're running out of time. The board meeting is next week, and we haven't even gotten half the town on board. People are scared—worried about what happens if they stick their necks out and nothing changes."

John nodded, his jaw tightening. "I know. But we can't stop now. Not when we're this close."

Grace hesitated. "What if it's not enough?"

John met her gaze, the weariness in his eyes matched by a quiet determination. "Then at least we'll know we tried. That we didn't let them take this without a fight."

Grace nodded slowly, her respect for him clear. "All right, John. Let's keep at it."

That night, as John sat alone in his office, the weight of the battle pressed down on him. He picked up Angelica's picture, his thumb brushing the frame.

"They don't believe we can do it," he murmured. "And maybe they're right."

But even as he spoke the words, he felt a flicker of resolve.

"You wouldn't give up," he said, his voice firmer now. "And I won't either."

He set the picture down, straightened his tie, and reached for the phone. The fight wasn't over—not yet.

The Last Day

The sun rose slowly over Jane's School on its final day, the early light casting a golden hue over the familiar building. The schoolyard, normally bustling with the excited chatter of children at this time of year, was quieter today. There was laughter, yes, but it carried an edge of sadness, a sense of something ending.

Inside, John Anderson stood in the main hallway, his hands clasped tightly behind his back. He had greeted children and teachers as they came in, offering his usual warm smile, but now he stood alone, taking in the details of the place that had been his second home for decades.

The worn lockers, the scuffed floors, the faint scent of chalk and books—it was all so familiar, yet today it felt heavy with finality.

The morning passed in a blur of activities. Teachers held small parties in their classrooms, children handed out hastily written notes and drawings, and the staff moved quietly through their routines, trying to make the day feel normal.

John made his rounds, visiting each classroom one last time.

In the music room, Ms. Carter led a group of children in a final song. As John stood in the doorway, she turned and smiled, motioning for him to join in.

He shook his head, but the children's earnest voices pulled him in, and before he knew it, he was singing along. The song ended with a round of applause, and John found himself choking back emotion as he thanked the children and Ms. Carter.

At lunchtime, the teachers gathered in the lounge for a potluck, their conversations subdued. Grace approached John with a plate of cookies, her expression soft.

"You've done everything you could, John," she said quietly.

He nodded, his jaw tight. "It wasn't enough."

Grace placed a hand on his arm. "It wasn't about winning or losing. It was about standing up for what mattered. And you did that. We all did."

John managed a faint smile. "Thanks, Grace."

The last bell rang at 3:00 PM, its echo lingering in the halls. Children spilled out of classrooms, their voices a mix of excitement for summer and sorrow for leaving.

John stood by the front doors as the students filed out, offering hugs and handshakes, his voice steady even as his heart broke.

"Goodbye, Mr. Anderson!"

"Thank you for everything, Mr. Anderson!"

"We'll miss you, Mr. Anderson!"

Each farewell cut deeper, but he returned every smile, every wave.

When the last bus pulled away, John stood on the front steps, watching it disappear down the road. The schoolyard fell silent, the only sound the rustling of leaves in the breeze.

Inside, the staff worked to pack up the last remnants of their classrooms. Tom Ferillo moved quietly through the halls, locking doors and turning off lights.

John returned to his office, the space feeling larger and emptier than ever. He sat at his desk, his eyes falling on the picture of Angelica.

"Well, Angelica," he said softly, "I did everything I could. I fought until there wasn't anything left to fight for."

He paused, running a hand over his face. "It's hard to walk away, but I think... I think you'd tell me it's time. Time to let go, even if it feels impossible."

The sound of a knock on the door pulled him from his thoughts.

Tom stood in the doorway, his hat in his hands. "Mr. Anderson, we're just about done."

John nodded, rising slowly. "Thanks, Tom."

The two men walked through the empty halls together, their footsteps echoing in the quiet.

At the front doors, John turned and looked back one last time. The sunlight streamed through the windows, casting long shadows across the floor.

"Goodbye, Jane's," he murmured.

Tom placed a hand on his shoulder. "It's not really gone, you know. Not as long as we remember."

John nodded, his throat tight. "You're right. Let's go."

As John stepped out into the fading light of the afternoon, he took a deep breath, the air filled with the scents of spring. The fight was over, and the loss was heavy, but in his heart, he knew Angelica would be proud of him.

He had given it everything. And now, he would find a way to move forward, carrying the spirit of Jane's School with him into whatever came next.

Goodbyes in the Gym

The gymnasium buzzed with activity, the sounds of folding chairs scraping against the floor and ladders creaking as volunteers strung garlands of winter greenery along the rafters. The old PA system emitted a faint hum, occasionally crackling as Tom Ferillo adjusted the microphone at the makeshift stage set up at the far end of the room.

"Testing, testing," Tom muttered into the mic. His voice echoed sharply, drawing a startled laugh from one of the younger volunteers.

"It works, Tom," Angelique, the town's librarian, called out from the rows of chairs she was arranging. "You don't have to scare everyone with it."

Tom rolled his eyes good-naturedly, stepping down from the stage. "Just making sure it doesn't cut out halfway through. Last thing we need is dead air during a speech."

At the back of the gym, a cluster of townspeople huddled near a long folding table covered in poster boards, photos, and handwritten notes. It was a makeshift timeline of the school's history, from its founding in the early 1900s to the present day.

"That's the first-grade class from 1957," Mrs. Whitman said, pointing to a black-and-white photo of smiling children lined up in front of the flagpole. "That was Angelica's first year, wasn't it?"

John Anderson stood nearby, his arms crossed as he studied the display. "It was," he said softly. "She brought so much energy to this place. The children adored her from the start."

Another man, Greg Hastings, a longtime resident and former school board member, shook his head. "It's a shame it's come to this. Closing the school feels like losing a part of ourselves."

"It's progress," a woman interjected, her tone brisk. It was Linda Marsh, the current school board chair. She gestured to a glossy flyer for the new consolidated school. "The new facility has everything these kids need—modern classrooms, better resources, and no crumbling ceilings to worry about. It's what's best for them."

"Best for them?" Greg shot back, his voice rising. "How is tearing down the heart of this community what's best for anyone? This school has been here for generations. My father went here, I went here, my kids went here. You can't replace that with shiny new buildings."

The debate rippled through the room, volunteers pausing in their tasks to join in.

"It's not just about the building," argued Helen Grant, a retired teacher. "It's about the connections we've built here. The memories, the traditions. You can't just uproot that and expect it to thrive somewhere else."

Linda sighed, her expression softening slightly. "I understand that, but times are changing. We have to think about what's practical, not just what's sentimental."

John stepped forward, his voice calm but firm. "Sentiment isn't a bad thing, Linda. It's what ties us to who we are, to what we value. But you're right about one thing—times are changing. The challenge isn't holding on to the past. It's finding a way to carry it with us into the future."

The room fell quiet for a moment, John's words cutting through the tension like a well-placed chime.

After a beat, Tom cleared his throat. "We've got a ceremony to plan, folks. Let's focus on making it something the kids and this community will remember."

The group nodded, returning to their tasks. Linda gave John a small, grateful smile before walking back to the stage to finalize the schedule for the farewell speeches.

As the afternoon wore on, the gymnasium began to take shape. A banner reading *Farewell, Jane's School: 1908–1985* hung above the stage, its letters painstakingly painted by the art teacher and her students. Rows of chairs faced the stage, and the timeline of photos and memories stretched across one wall like a tapestry of shared history.

John wandered to the back of the room, where a small table held a display dedicated to Angelica. It featured photos of her at the piano, her concert programs, and even one of the first sheet music books she'd used when she started teaching.

Tom joined him, hands in his pockets. "She'd have loved this, wouldn't she?"

John smiled faintly, his gaze lingering on a photo of Angelica leading the school choir. "She would have. And she'd be the first to remind us that endings are just beginnings in disguise."

Tom nodded, his expression thoughtful. "Guess it's up to us to figure out what that beginning looks like."

"It is," John said, his voice steady. "And it starts with remembering what this place means to all of us."

As the sun dipped lower outside, casting a warm glow through the gymnasium windows, the community worked together to prepare their farewell—a ceremony that would honor not just the school, but the spirit that had made it a home for so many.

Progress vs. Nostalgia: The Debate

The principal's office had always been a place of quiet reflection for John Anderson, but today it felt smaller, almost stifling. The shelves, once lined with meticulously arranged textbooks and binders, now stood half-empty, their contents packed into boxes in preparation for his retirement.

Across the desk from him sat Emily Carter, a young official from the district, her sharp blazer and tablet a stark contrast to the office's worn furniture and faint smell of chalk dust.

Emily smiled politely, though her demeanor carried an air of efficiency. "Mr. Anderson, I appreciate you taking the time to meet with me. I wanted to go over the logistics for the school's closure and the transition to the new facility."

John nodded, leaning back slightly in his chair. "Of course. I'm here to help however I can."

Emily tapped at her tablet, scrolling through her notes. "It seems like most of the arrangements are in place. The students have already been assigned to their new school, and the district has allocated resources to ensure a smooth adjustment."

"Efficient," John said, his tone even but not without a hint of irony.

Emily caught the subtlety and looked up. "I understand this must be difficult for you, Mr. Anderson. You've been here for decades, and I can only imagine the memories tied to this place."

"Memories aren't the problem," John replied. "It's what happens to the people who made those memories."

Emily folded her hands, resting them on the desk. "Change is always hard. But the new school offers so many opportunities—modern facilities, better technology, specialized programs. It's what today's students need to thrive in the world we live in now."

John studied her for a moment, his weathered face calm but thoughtful. "And what about the world we're leaving behind?"

Emily hesitated, clearly trying to find the right words. "I don't think it's about leaving anything behind. It's about building on it, evolving."

John nodded slowly. "I've heard that word a lot lately—'evolving.' But evolution isn't just about moving forward. It's about adapting while holding onto what matters."

Emily frowned slightly, leaning forward. "Are you saying the new school won't hold onto what matters?"

"I'm saying it's easy to lose sight of what matters when the focus is on what's new," John said. His voice was calm, but his gaze was steady. "A school isn't just walls and technology. It's the connections, the traditions, the people. Those things don't come with a blueprint."

Emily sighed, her tone softening. "I'm not trying to diminish what this school has meant to the community. But we have to think about the future. We're preparing these kids for a world that's constantly changing."

John leaned forward, resting his hands on the desk. "And how do you prepare them for the things that don't change? For kindness, resilience, community? Those lessons aren't found in modern facilities. They're found in people, in places that feel like home."

Emily's eyes softened, and for a moment, the efficiency in her demeanor gave way to something more genuine. "You're right. Those things are important. But isn't it possible to carry them forward? To create a new sense of home in a new place?"

John smiled faintly, his tone warmer now. "It's possible. But it takes more than bricks and mortar. It takes intention. And it takes people who care enough to remember what came before."

Emily leaned back, a small smile breaking across her face. "You're not what I expected, Mr. Anderson. Not after our last meeting, I mean."

"And what did you expect?" he asked, raising an eyebrow.

"More resistance to change," she admitted. "But I see now that's not the case. You're not against change—you're against losing what matters in the process."

John nodded. "Exactly. Progress isn't the enemy. Forgetting is."

Emily tilted her head, her expression thoughtful. "Then maybe that's something we can work on. Finding a way to honor the legacy of Jane's School while moving forward."

"I'd like that," John said, his voice steady. "And I think Angelica would have liked it, too."

"Angelica?" Emily asked.

John smiled wistfully. "My late wife. She taught music here for years. She was the soul of this place."

Emily returned his smile, a flicker of respect in her eyes. "Then let's make sure her spirit is part of what comes next."

As Emily stood to leave, she extended her hand. John shook it firmly, his heart lighter than it had been in weeks.

"Thank you for your time, Mr. Anderson," she said.

"Thank you for listening," he replied.

As the door closed behind her, John glanced around the office, his gaze lingering on the boxes and the empty shelves. For the first time in a long while, he felt a glimmer of hope—not just for the school's past, but for its future as well.

A Picture Worth a Thousand Memories

The late afternoon sun slanted through the tall windows of the principal's office, illuminating the dust motes swirling in the air. John Anderson stood by the desk, sorting through the last remnants of decades spent in this room. Cardboard boxes filled with folders, old attendance records, and forgotten memorabilia lined the walls, their contents waiting to be packed away or discarded.

He opened a drawer at the bottom of the desk, one he hadn't touched in years. It groaned in protest, the metal scraping against the frame, and John crouched down, peering into its shadowed depths.

At first, it seemed like nothing but papers—forgotten schedules, outdated forms, and handwritten notes—but then his hand brushed against something firmer, its edges stiff and distinct. He pulled it free and found himself holding a photograph, its black-and-white surface worn smooth with age.

John straightened, the photo trembling slightly in his hands as he turned it toward the light.

The image showed Angelica seated at the piano, her head tilted slightly as she smiled at someone just out of frame. Beside her stood Bobby Ferillo, his violin tucked under his chin, his bow poised mid-stroke. His expression was one of pure focus, his youthful confidence practically leaping off the image.

They were in the music room—he recognized the old bulletin board in the background and the sunlight filtering through the tall windows, creating soft halos around them both.

John exhaled slowly, sinking into the chair behind the desk.

The memories rushed back unbidden.

He could hear Angelica's laughter, the way it had filled the room as Bobby tried to play a particularly tricky passage. "Almost there," she had said, her tone always encouraging, never critical. "One more time, Bobby—you've got this."

And Bobby had. He'd mastered the piece with Angelica's patient guidance, his talent growing sharper with each passing day.

John ran his thumb gently along the edge of the photograph. Bobby had been so young then, his potential limitless. And Angelica—he swallowed hard as he looked at her radiant smile—had been at her most vibrant, her love for the music and the children she taught shining in every line of her face.

A soft knock on the door broke his reverie.

"Mr. Anderson?" Tom Ferillo stepped inside, his brow furrowing when he saw John sitting there, the photograph in his hands. "You all right?"

John looked up, offering a faint smile. "I found something, Tom. Something I hadn't thought about in years."

Tom crossed the room, leaning over to get a better look. His breath caught when he saw the image.

"That's Bobby," he said softly, his voice tinged with awe. He traced the air above the photo, not quite touching it. "And Miss Thompson."

John nodded. "She loved teaching him. Said he had a gift—one that deserved to be shared with the world."

Tom swallowed hard, his jaw tightening. "He always said she believed in him more than he believed in himself."

"She believed in all her students," John said, his voice distant as he stared at the photo. "But there was something about Bobby... and about her. They brought out the best in each other."

Tom sat on the edge of the desk, his hands clasped tightly. "I think about him a lot, you know. About what he could've done if... if things had been different."

"So do I," John admitted. "But I also think about what he did while he was here. The way he inspired people—just like Angelica did."

Tom's eyes shimmered, though he quickly blinked the tears away. "That's what this school was, wasn't it? A place where people like Bobby and Miss Thompson could make their mark. Where they could become something more."

John smiled faintly, his thumb brushing against Angelica's image. "It still is, Tom. And as long as we carry their stories with us, it always will be."

For a long moment, the two men sat in silence, the weight of the photograph binding them together in shared memory.

Finally, John set the photo carefully on the desk. "We should add this to the display in the gym," he said. "People should see it—remember what this school was, and what it gave to all of us."

Tom nodded. "I'll frame it. It deserves that much."

As Tom left the room, carrying the photograph like a sacred relic, John leaned back in his chair.

For the first time in weeks, he felt a sense of peace. The photograph was more than just an image—it was a reminder of the love and brilliance that had defined Jane's School, and a testament to the people who had made it extraordinary.

And in that moment, John knew that even as the school's doors closed, its spirit would endure.

An Evening of Tears and Tributes

The gymnasium was packed, every chair filled with townspeople, teachers, and former students, while others stood along the walls, spilling into the hallways. Strings of twinkling lights looped across the rafters, casting a soft, warm glow over the room. The scent of pine from the garlands draped along the stage mingled with the faint aroma of coffee and baked goods set up at the refreshment tables.

At the front of the room, a large banner stretched across the stage: *Farewell, Jane's School: 1908–1985*. Below it, a timeline display of photos, newspaper clippings, and handwritten notes paid tribute to decades of memories.

John Anderson stood off to the side of the stage, his cane in hand. He surveyed the room, his heart heavy yet full. Everywhere he looked, he saw familiar faces—former students who now had children of their own, teachers he'd worked alongside, and townsfolk whose lives had been shaped by this school.

Tom Ferillo approached, adjusting his tie awkwardly. "It's quite the crowd, huh?"

John smiled faintly. "It is. I didn't realize how many people would come."

"They're here for you, Mr. Anderson," Tom said, his voice carrying quiet admiration.

Linda Marsh, the school board chair, stepped to the microphone, tapping it gently to quiet the hum of conversation.

"Good evening, everyone," she began, her voice steady. "Thank you all for joining us tonight to honor Jane's School and, of course, the man who has been its heart and soul for the past twenty-eight years, Mr. John Anderson."

The crowd erupted into applause, the sound filling the gymnasium and echoing off the walls. John shifted uncomfortably, his modesty making him resist the spotlight.

Linda continued, her tone warm. "This school has been more than just a place of learning. It's been a cornerstone of our community, a place where generations have grown, dreamed, and found their paths. Tonight, we're here to celebrate its legacy and the incredible man who helped shape it."

One by one, speakers took the stage to share their memories.

Helen Grant, a retired teacher, spoke about John's dedication to his staff. "John was the kind of principal who knew how to listen. Whether it was a parent concerned about their child or a teacher struggling with a new curriculum, he always made time for us. He believed in this school—and in all of us."

Greg Hastings, a former school board member, recounted a time when budget cuts threatened the arts program. "John fought tooth and nail to keep music and art alive here. He told us, 'These kids deserve more than just the basics. They deserve inspiration.' And he was right."

Angelique, the town librarian, stepped forward next. "I'll never forget the day I was struggling with my reading as a kid, and Mr. Anderson found me crying in the library. He sat with me, read a chapter of my book aloud, and told me I could finish it if I took it one page at a time. That's the kind of man he is—someone who believes in the power of small steps."

Finally, Linda returned to the microphone. "Before we close, we'd like to invite Mr. Anderson to the stage to say a few words."

The crowd burst into applause again, many standing as John made his way to the podium, his cane clicking softly against the floor.

He took a deep breath, gripping the edges of the podium as he looked out at the sea of faces.

"I've never been good at speeches," he began, his voice slightly rough. "But I'll do my best."

The crowd chuckled softly, the warmth in the room spreading.

"This school has been my life," John continued. "Not just because it's where I worked, but because it's where I learned what it means to be part of something bigger than yourself. Every student who walked these halls, every teacher who poured their heart into their lessons, every parent who trusted us with their children—they all built this place. I just had the privilege of being a part of it."

He paused, his throat tightening as he glanced at the timeline display and the photo of Angelica. "Jane's School isn't just a building. It's a home. A family. And while its doors may close, its spirit will live on—in the lives we've touched, and in the memories we carry."

The crowd was silent, many wiping tears from their eyes.

"Thank you," John said, his voice breaking slightly. "For letting me be part of this. For letting me be part of you."

The gymnasium was alive with applause, the echoes bouncing off the walls as John Anderson stepped down from the stage. The farewell ceremony had been moving so far—filled with heartfelt memories and quiet reflections—but beneath the surface, tension simmered.

John had just taken his seat near the front when the murmurs began. They started at the back of the room, a low buzz of whispered conversations and sideways glances. Soon, a voice rose above the rest, sharp and defiant.

"This school shouldn't be closing!"

The crowd quieted instantly, heads swiveling toward the source. It was Greg Hastings, a former school board member, standing near the photo timeline with his arms crossed. His face was red, his tone angry but controlled.

"This place is the heart of our town," Greg continued, his voice gaining strength. "We've just spent the evening talking about how much it's meant to all of us—how many lives it's shaped. And now we're letting it go? For what? A shiny new building miles away?"

Linda Marsh, seated near the stage, rose quickly and moved toward the microphone. She spoke with practiced calm, though her jaw was tight.

"Greg," she said, her voice cutting through the murmurs, "we've had this discussion before. The decision to close Jane's School wasn't made lightly. The new facility will provide better opportunities for our students—modern resources, safer infrastructure, things this building simply can't offer anymore."

"But at what cost, Linda?" Greg shot back, stepping closer to the front of the room. "Do you think a modern classroom can replace the sense of community this school gives us? Do you think it can replace decades of history?"

Others in the audience began to chime in, their voices creating a growing cacophony.

"He's right!" shouted a middle-aged woman. "My kids don't need fancy computers—they need teachers who know them, a school that feels like home!"

"Home doesn't fix broken roofs," another voice countered. "Or pay for heating bills in the winter!"

"What about tradition?" someone else called out. "What about keeping something alive that's been here for generations?"

"Tradition doesn't prepare kids for the future!"

The volume rose as arguments broke out across the gymnasium, the unity of the evening unraveling into heated debates.

John, seated near the stage, leaned on his cane as he slowly stood. His voice, though soft, carried weight as he spoke.

"Enough."

The single word cut through the chaos like a bell, and the room fell silent, all eyes turning toward him.

John moved toward the microphone, his steps slow but deliberate. Linda stepped aside, her expression a mixture of relief and apprehension.

John gripped the edges of the podium, looking out over the crowd.

"I understand your frustration," he began, his voice steady. "And I understand your anger. This school is more than just a building. It's a place where we've laughed, learned, struggled, and grown together. It's been a home for so many of us. And saying goodbye to that is painful."

He paused, letting the weight of his words settle over the room.

"But we can't let that pain tear us apart. Change is never easy. And yes, it's fair to question it, to mourn what we're losing. But we have to remember why we're here tonight—to honor this school, its legacy, and what it's given to each of us."

Greg stepped forward, his expression still tense. "And what happens to that legacy, John? Does it get packed away in a box like the photos on that wall?"

John met his gaze, his tone firm but kind. "No, Greg. That legacy lives on— in us, in the people who carry its lessons and memories forward. The building may close, but the spirit of Jane's School doesn't end here. It continues in every student who walked these halls, every teacher who gave their all, and every person in this room who believes in what this place stands for."

The room was quiet now, the earlier tension replaced by a reflective stillness.

Linda stepped forward again, her voice softer than before. "John's right. The new school doesn't erase what this one has meant to us. But it's our job to make sure that legacy continues—to take what we've built here and make it part of what comes next."

Greg hesitated, then gave a slow nod, the fight in his posture softening.

John turned back to the crowd. "This isn't the end. It's a new chapter. And just like we've done for generations, we'll face it together."

The applause that followed was hesitant at first, but soon grew into a wave of agreement. The tension in the room eased, replaced by a sense of shared understanding.

The ceremony continued. John returned to his seat, his heart heavy but hopeful. The storm of emotions and conflict was far from over, but for now, the community was united in honoring what mattered most—the heart of Jane's School and the people who would carry it forward.

As the ceremony wound down, John stood near the stage, shaking hands and exchanging hugs with a steady stream of people.

"You'll never really leave this place, Mr. Anderson," a former student said, her voice filled with emotion. "You'll always be part of it."

John smiled, his heart full. "And it'll always be part of me."

The Storm Outside, the Calm Within

The sky had turned a deep, restless gray by the time the farewell ceremony ended. Outside the gymnasium, the first raindrops spattered against the windows, leaving streaks that gleamed faintly in the dim light.

John Anderson stood near the door, his cane resting against his leg as he shook hands and exchanged goodbyes with the last of the attendees. Each handshake, each word of thanks and lingering glance, felt like a small goodbye to the life he had known for so long.

Tom Ferillo approached, his jacket slung over one shoulder, his expression tired but warm.

"You sure you don't need a ride home, Mr. Anderson?" Tom asked, gesturing toward the parking lot where the wind was beginning to whip up stray leaves.

John smiled faintly, shaking his head. "No, thank you, Tom. I think I'll stay a little while longer. Just to walk the halls one more time."

Tom hesitated, his brow furrowing. "Storm's coming in fast. Don't wait too long, okay?"

"I won't," John assured him.

With a nod, Tom gave him a firm handshake before heading out into the growing storm.

The gymnasium was quiet now, the echoes of the farewell ceremony lingering faintly in the air. The folding chairs were stacked neatly against the walls, and the timeline display still stretched across one side of the room, its photos and mementos softly illuminated by the string lights overhead.

John walked slowly across the floor, his cane tapping softly against the polished wood. His steps carried him to the stage, where the banner reading *Farewell, Jane's School: 1908–1985* hung above the empty podium.

He reached out, his fingers brushing the edge of the podium. It was still warm from where he had gripped it earlier, delivering what might have been his last speech to the community he loved.

The rain began to fall harder, drumming against the roof and windows.

Leaving the gym, John made his way down the main hallway. The light from the frosted windows was dim, casting long shadows across the worn tile floor.

He paused outside the music room, his hand hovering over the door handle. Slowly, he pushed it open and stepped inside. The piano stood in its familiar corner, the same place it had been since the day Angelica arrived. The faint scent of dust and aged wood filled the air, mingling with the memory of her presence.

John sat on the bench, his hands resting on his knees. The room felt heavier now, the storm outside lending an almost oppressive weight to the silence.

"You'd love this storm, wouldn't you?" he murmured, his voice barely audible over the rain. "Said it was the best time to think. To let the chaos outside help you find the calm inside."

He reached out, his fingers brushing the keys. A single, soft note rang out, pure and clear, before fading into the quiet.

The rain intensified, and the sound of thunder rolled in the distance as John left the music room. The hallways felt endless, each step carrying him past lockers and classrooms that held decades of memories.

When he reached the front doors, he stopped, resting his hand on the cool metal frame. Outside, the two great maples swayed in the wind, their bare branches stark against the darkening sky.

The raindrops hitting the glass seemed almost rhythmic, like the ticking of a clock marking the passage of time.

John stood there for a long moment, the storm swirling around him, the echoes of the day replaying in his mind. The laughter, the tears, the arguments—it had all been part of saying goodbye, part of acknowledging the end of something he had poured his life into.

Finally, he turned away from the doors, his steps deliberate as he moved deeper into the school. The building groaned faintly under the weight of the storm, the sound blending with the rising wind.

The gathering was over. The farewells had been said.

Now, it was just John and the empty halls, the storm outside mirroring the emotions churning within him.

Lightning Strikes (Metaphorically)

The storm outside raged with unrelenting ferocity, the rain hammering against the windows and the wind howling through every crevice of Jane's School. The power had flickered a few times before finally giving out, plunging the old building into shadows interrupted only by the flashes of lightning.

John Anderson stood in the main hallway, his cane steadying him as he stared into the dimness. The storm outside seemed to echo the storm within him—loud, chaotic, and unyielding.

He moved forward slowly, his footsteps soft against the worn tile. Each flash of lightning illuminated the lockers, the bulletin boards, the doors of classrooms he had once known so well. The shadows cast by the brief bursts of light seemed to flicker with life, as if the building itself were caught in the storm's grasp.

John paused in front of the fourth-grade classroom, his hand brushing the dusty glass of the door's window. For decades, this had been his room, the place where he had tried to teach children not just facts and figures but the value of curiosity, resilience, and kindness.

He had resisted the school's closure with everything he had. He had fought against the tides of change, clinging to the walls and halls of this place like they were the only things that mattered.

But now, standing in the silent darkness, he realized how small the building felt without the people who had filled it with life.

A brilliant flash of lightning split the sky outside, its light flooding the hallway for a heartbeat. In that instant, John saw the lockers, the classrooms, and the entryway with perfect clarity. And in the fleeting illumination, he thought he saw something more—a flicker of memory brought vividly to life.

The hallway wasn't empty anymore. It was alive, filled with the echoes of students running to class, teachers calling out reminders, and laughter bouncing off the walls.

And there was Angelica, standing in the distance by the music room, her auburn hair glowing in the light, her hands clasped as she smiled at him.

The light faded, and the shadows returned, leaving John alone in the hallway. But the image of Angelica lingered, her presence as vivid as the thunder rolling overhead.

Her words came back to him, as clear as if she were standing beside him. *"Change isn't the enemy, John. It's what keeps us moving forward. What we've built here doesn't end—it carries on, in the people we've touched and the lives we've shaped."*

John gripped his cane tightly, his throat constricting. He had been so afraid of letting go, so afraid of losing what Jane's School had meant to him. But now he understood.

It wasn't the building that mattered. It was the spirit of what they had created together—the connections, the lessons, the love. That was what Angelica had wanted him to see. That was her message all along.

The storm outside began to ease, the rain softening, the wind less insistent. John took a deep breath, his shoulders relaxing for the first time in days.

He turned, heading back toward the music room. When he reached it, he pushed the door open and stepped inside, the faint light from the windows casting a silvery glow over the piano.

He placed his hand on the keys, a small smile breaking through the sorrow in his heart. "I hear you, Angelica," he said softly. "I understand now."

As he left the music room, the hallway felt different—lighter, less burdened. The storm had passed, both outside and within.

For the first time, John felt ready to move forward, to embrace the change he had resisted for so long. Angelica's message wasn't just about letting go—it was about carrying their legacy into the future.

And now, he knew he could.

The Morning After

The next morning dawned clear and bright, as if the world itself didn't realize what had been lost. John Anderson sat in his office, staring at the bare walls where photographs and certificates had once hung. The desk, too, was nearly empty, save for his favorite fountain pen and a few stray papers. The end of Jane's School had come and gone, but the ache in his chest remained sharp.

A knock at the door startled him from his thoughts.

"Come in," he called, his voice weary.

The door opened, and Emily Carter stepped inside. She was dressed sharply as always, but her usual brisk demeanor was tempered with something softer.

"Good morning, Mr. Anderson," she said, her tone tentative.

"Miss Carter," John replied, leaning back in his chair. "To what do I owe the pleasure?"

Emily hesitated for a moment, then stepped closer, her clipboard held loosely at her side. "I was at the ceremony last night."

John raised an eyebrow. "I didn't see you there."

"I stayed in the back," she admitted. "I didn't think it was my place to make my presence known. But I needed to see it for myself."

John nodded slowly, waiting for her to continue.

"I wanted to thank you," she said, her voice steady but sincere. "For how you handled things. The dissent could have turned the evening into something ugly, but you saved it. You reminded everyone what really mattered, and you did it with grace."

John's lips twitched into a faint smile. "Grace, huh? Angelica would've laughed at that one."

Emily smiled, though it was tinged with regret. "I also wanted to apologize. I thought I understood your resistance when we first spoke, but I didn't—not really. Last night, I saw it. I saw what this school means to you, to this community. I'm sorry for how it all played out."

John leaned forward, his hands resting on the desk. "What's done is done, Miss Carter. Apologies won't bring the school back."

She nodded, her gaze dropping to the clipboard in her hands. "No, they won't. But I came here because I think you deserve to hear it face-to-face—and because I have a proposition for you."

John raised an eyebrow. "A proposition?"

Emily took a seat across from him, setting her clipboard on the desk. "The school may be closed, but the district hasn't decided what to do with the building yet. There's talk of repurposing it—turning it into a community center or leasing it out for other educational purposes. But that's a long process, and in the meantime, we need someone to oversee the wind-down."

"And you think that someone should be me?" John asked, his tone even.

"I do," Emily said. "You know this school better than anyone. You care about it more than anyone. Who better to make sure it's taken care of during this transition?"

John studied her for a long moment, his expression unreadable.

"It would be a part-time role," Emily continued. "You'd have the freedom to step back if you wanted to, but you'd also have the opportunity to ensure the building is used in a way that honors its legacy."

John leaned back in his chair, his gaze drifting to the window. Outside, the spring breeze rustled the leaves of the great maples, their new growth a reminder of the cycles of life.

"I'm not sure I'm the right man for the job," he said finally.

Emily tilted her head, her tone softening. "I think you are. And I think you know it, too."

The office fell quiet, save for the faint ticking of the clock on the wall. John thought of the ceremony, the faces of the students and teachers, the echoes of Angelica's voice in his mind.

Finally, he met Emily's gaze. "I'll consider it."

Her shoulders relaxed slightly, relief evident in her expression. "That's all I can ask, Mr. Anderson."

As she stood to leave, she extended her hand. John hesitated for a moment, then took it, his grip firm.

"Thank you," she said quietly.

He nodded, his voice steady. "We'll see where this goes, Miss Carter. But if I do this, I'll do it my way."

Emily smiled faintly. "I wouldn't expect anything less."

After Emily left, John remained in his office, the offer lingering in his mind. The fight for Jane's School was over, but maybe there was still work to be done—one last chance to shape its legacy.

He looked at Angelica's picture on the desk, her smile as steady and encouraging as ever.

"What do you think?" he murmured.

The sunlight streaming through the window seemed to brighten, casting a warm glow over the room.

John exhaled deeply, a faint smile tugging at the corners of his mouth. "All right, Angelica. One more chapter. Let's see where it takes us."

And with that, John Anderson picked up his pen, ready to write the next part of Jane's School's story.

Lessons from the Maples

1986

The drizzle clung to John Anderson's coat as he stood near the flagpole, staring up at the two great maples that framed Jane's School. The wind had slowed from its earlier fury, but it still whipped through the trees, shaking loose droplets of water that glittered faintly in the dim light.

The maples had been there long before John's time. They were planted, he'd been told, when the school first opened in 1908—a symbol of strength and growth for the fledgling institution. Over the decades, they had stood as silent witnesses to the lives that passed beneath their branches.

Now, as the storm's remnants swirled around them, the trees seemed to sway in rhythm with the building's quiet resilience.

John's gaze lingered on the trunks, their rough bark marked with deep grooves and scars. He could see where lightning had struck one during a storm in the early '60s, leaving a dark streak down its side. He remembered how Angelica had insisted on saving the tree, calling in a specialist from the next county over.

"Trees like this don't just grow overnight, John," she'd said, her voice firm but full of wonder. "They've earned their place here, just like we have."

And now, despite the storm's battering winds and relentless rain, the maples stood firm. Some smaller branches lay scattered on the ground, their leaves long gone with the autumn's passing, but the core of the trees—their unyielding trunks, their network of roots—remained steadfast.

The wind picked up, bending the maples' upper branches almost to their breaking point. John instinctively tightened his grip on his cane, watching as the trees weathered the assault.

For a fleeting moment, he saw himself in the trees. Time had tested him, just as it had tested them. The loss of Angelica, the closing of the school, the ache of old age—they were his storms, stripping away what seemed essential and leaving him raw and uncertain.

But the maples showed him something he hadn't considered. They didn't fight the wind. They bent with it, swaying but never snapping. Their strength wasn't in resisting the storm—it was in enduring it.

"They adapt," John murmured aloud, his voice carried away by the breeze.

His thoughts wandered to the roots buried deep beneath the ground. He'd once read that trees like the maples could survive because of their interconnected roots, which supported each other and shared resources in times of need.

It wasn't just the trees' own strength that kept them standing—it was their connection to one another.

The realization struck him with quiet clarity. That was what Jane's School had been. Not just a building, but a network of roots—a foundation that had supported the lives of everyone who passed through its doors.

The school was closing, yes, but the roots remained. The lessons taught, the relationships formed, the love and care poured into the students—they would endure, just like the trees.

A gust of wind sent a shiver down John's spine, and he adjusted his coat, glancing at the branches again.

"Twenty-nine years," he said softly. "And they've been here for all of them."

The wind eased for a moment, and in the stillness, John could almost hear Angelica's voice. *"It's not about holding on, John. It's about standing strong, even when the storms come."*

He smiled faintly, the ache in his chest loosening. "I hear you, Angelica. I miss you."

As the drizzle turned to mist, John took a step forward, placing a hand on the rough bark of one of the maples. It felt solid beneath his palm, its surface cool and damp but alive.

"Thank you," he said, his words barely audible.

He stayed there a moment longer, letting the quiet of the post-storm world settle around him. The maples swayed gently in the breeze, their resilience speaking more clearly than words ever could.

When John finally turned to go, he carried a new understanding with him. The storms would come, but like the maples, he could bend without breaking. The school's legacy, like the trees' roots, would remain—alive and steady, even as the winds of change swept through.

And as he walked back toward the school doors, the maples stood tall behind him, a living metaphor for the enduring strength of life, love, and connection.

Tom's Outstretched Hand

The downpour had quieted into a steady drizzle by the time Tom Ferillo pushed open the doors to Jane's School. The wind still tugged at his jacket, and his boots squeaked faintly on the damp floor as he stepped inside.

"Mr. Anderson?" Tom called, his voice echoing in the empty hallway.

There was no immediate response, only the faint creak of the building settling in the storm's aftermath. Tom frowned, pulling his cap lower against the chill. He had offered to stay earlier, but John had insisted on being alone. Now, with the storm's ferocity abated, worry had brought Tom back.

Tom walked slowly down the hallway, his flashlight casting soft beams against the worn lockers and scuffed tiles. When he reached the music room, the door was open, and he paused, peering inside.

"Mr. Anderson?" he called again, stepping into the familiar space.

John was there, sitting on the piano bench, his hand resting lightly on the keys. He didn't seem startled by Tom's arrival; instead, he looked up with a faint smile, his face softer than it had been earlier in the evening.

"Tom," John said, his voice low but steady. "You didn't have to come back."

Tom crossed the room, his boots leaving faint prints on the dusty floor. "I know," he said simply. "But I figured you shouldn't be here alone, not in this weather."

Tom sat on a nearby chair, setting his flashlight on the piano. "You all right?"

John nodded slowly. "I think I am. The storm gave me time to think... to see things more clearly."

Tom tilted his head, studying the older man. "See what?"

John tapped a single note on the piano, its sound ringing softly in the quiet room. "That holding on too tightly can keep you from moving forward. Angelica tried to teach me that before she passed. Took me a while to understand it."

Tom leaned forward, his elbows resting on his knees. "It's not easy to let go of something that's been part of you for so long."

"No, it's not," John agreed. "But letting go doesn't mean forgetting. It doesn't mean leaving it behind."

Tom nodded thoughtfully, his expression softening. "Angelica would've liked that."

John smiled faintly. "She would've."

The two men sat in comfortable silence for a moment, the room filled with the faint sound of rain tapping against the windows.

Finally, Tom stood, his movements slow but purposeful. "Come on, Mr. Anderson. Let me help you out of here. We can lock up together."

John hesitated, his gaze sweeping the music room one last time.

"All right," he said, standing with the aid of his cane. "But first, let's make sure this room is locked properly. Angelica would've wanted it that way."

Tom chuckled softly. "She always did have a thing for keeping things in order."

As they walked together through the halls, Tom kept a steadying hand near John, their footsteps echoing in the quiet. The building felt different now—less like an empty shell and more like a vessel filled with memories, ready to carry them forward.

When they reached the front doors, Tom glanced at John. "You ready?"

John nodded, his grip on his cane firm. "Yes. I'm ready."

With Tom's support, they stepped out into the rain, the school's doors closing behind them. The worst of the storm had passed, but its lessons remained, etched in their hearts as they walked together into the night.

Locking the Past Away

The cold metal of the padlock felt heavy in John Anderson's hand. He turned it over, the grooves worn smooth from years of use. The red doors of the school's main entrance loomed before him, their once-bright paint faded to a dull, peeling crimson. A thin layer of frost clung to the edges, catching the early morning light.

John's breath fogged in the crisp winter air as he stared at the lock, the key resting in his palm. He knew he had unlocked and locked these doors countless times over the years, but today the action felt monumental, as if the simple turn of the key might undo everything that had come before.

He slipped the key into the padlock, twisting it with a click. The chain fell loose, clinking against the ground. Pushing open the doors, John stepped inside, the sudden silence of the empty hallway enveloping him.

The cold followed him, seeping through his coat as he walked past the rows of lockers, his cane tapping softly against the floor. He paused in front of a classroom, its door closed and secured with another padlock.

His fingers brushed the handle, the chill of the metal biting his skin. He had once promised himself he'd never let these doors be locked, that the school would always remain open—a beacon for the town, a place where children could dream, learn, and grow.

But now, they were locked, not just against the cold but against time itself.

John leaned heavily on his cane, his shoulders slumping. "It wasn't supposed to end like this," he murmured to no one in particular.

The echoes of his voice carried through the hall, faint reminders of the life that had once filled these walls.

His thoughts drifted to the children who had passed through these doors, their laughter ringing like a distant memory. The lockers had once been decorated with stickers and crayon drawings; the classrooms had hummed with the energy of young minds.

He could almost see them—Bobby Ferillo at the piano, his fingers deft and sure under Angelica's watchful eye. Little Clara Mayfield from his own fourth-grade class, always eager with her hand raised. Even Tom Ferillo, years before he had returned as a custodian, struggling with a math problem but never giving up.

They were all gone now, scattered to the winds of time, just as Angelica was.

John's grip on the door handle tightened. The padlock stared back at him, a symbol of the school's finality.

He raised his cane and tapped it lightly against the metal. The sound echoed sharply, breaking the stillness.

"It's just a lock," he told himself, though the weight in his chest made it feel like much more. "It doesn't mean it's all gone."

But he wasn't sure he believed his own words.

With a deep sigh, John turned back toward the entrance. As he walked, the cold seemed to press in closer, the hallway longer than he remembered.

When he reached the front doors, he picked up the chain and began threading it back into place. Each loop around the handles felt heavier than the last, each clink of the chain echoing like a hammer striking an anvil.

When he slid the padlock into place and snapped it shut, the sound was final.

He stood there for a moment, staring at the locked doors, his breath visible in the frigid air.

"It's not just a building," he said aloud, as if to reassure himself. "It's the people, the memories, the lives it touched. That's what matters."

His voice sounded hollow in the empty space, and for a moment, doubt crept in.

But then he turned and looked out through the glass, past the flagpole and toward the two great maples that stood at the entrance. Their bare branches swayed gently in the wind, steadfast against the season.

The padlocks couldn't hold back time, but they couldn't erase it either.

With a final glance at the doors, John stepped into the winter air, his cane tapping a steady rhythm as he walked away. The school might be locked, but its memories—and its spirit—remained open in his heart.

Homemade Cinnamon Rolls

1987

The afternoon sun streamed through the kitchen window, catching the dust motes as they floated lazily in the warm spring air. The scent of freshly brewed coffee lingered, mingling with the faint aroma of Clara's homemade cinnamon rolls cooling on the counter.

John Anderson sat at the small kitchen table, listening to Clara hum softly as she worked. Her hands moved deftly as she arranged plates and cups, a task that seemed second nature to her.

"James and Nichole really wanted to come, you know," Clara said, breaking the silence.

John looked up from his coffee, a faint smile tugging at his lips. "They've got their own lives now. James with his new family, Nichole planning a wedding—it's how it should be."

Clara turned to face him, a knowing look in her eyes. "They're not too busy for you, John. They just couldn't make it this time. You know how much they care about you."

John nodded but didn't reply, his gaze dropping to the table.

"They talk about you all the time," Clara continued, setting a plate of rolls on the table. "James especially. He's excited about the baby, but he keeps wondering if he'll be as good a father as you were a mentor to him and Bobby."

The mention of Bobby made John's chest tighten, but he managed a small smile. "James doesn't give himself enough credit. He's going to be a great father."

Clara sat across from him, folding her hands on the table. "And Nichole—she's using all those lessons she learned from you and Angelica. You should hear the way she talks about her students. You've left your mark on both of them, John. Don't ever doubt that."

The sound of a car pulling into the driveway drew their attention. Clara glanced toward the window, her expression brightening. "Edward's back, finally."

John stood, his knees stiff with the wear of years but his stride steady as he moved toward the door.

"He meant to come in and say hi before," Clara said, brushing crumbs from her hands. "But, you know him—probably got caught up looking at the maples or fiddling with the old latch on the shed."

John nodded, keeping his thoughts to himself. Edward's distractions weren't new, but they always carried an unspoken weight—half an apology, half a promise to do better.

Edward stepped out of the car with his usual unhurried grace, his tall frame unmistakable even after all these years. As the sunlight caught his silver hair, his sharp features softened briefly, caught between formality and fondness.

"John," Edward said, extending a hand as he approached.

John shook it firmly, a smile breaking through his usually reserved demeanor. "Edward. Good to see you."

Behind Edward, his wife, Clara, was already reaching into the trunk for a picnic basket and a bouquet of fresh flowers. She waved cheerfully. "Don't just stand there, you two. Help me with this, or we'll be here all day."

Later, as the four of them sat in the backyard under the shade of the budding maple trees, the conversation turned to Angelica.

"Every time I come here," Edward said, his voice softer than usual, "I feel like I can hear her laughing. She had a way of making everything seem brighter."

John nodded, his gaze distant. "She was the best of us."

Edward hesitated, then leaned forward, his tone more earnest. "John, I'll admit—I haven't always understood why Angelica loved this place so much. But seeing it now, hearing how much you've done to keep it alive... I get it."

John looked at him, surprised by the uncharacteristic warmth in Edward's voice.

"I haven't always been the easiest person to get along with," Edward continued, "but I want you to know—I respect what you've done here. And what you've done for Clara, for James, for Nichole. You've been more than just family. You've been a rock."

The words settled over the group, mending unspoken tensions that had lingered for years.

Clara reached out, covering John's hand with hers. "And you've been our connection to Angelica. Don't ever forget how much you mean to us."

John's throat tightened, but he managed a nod. "Thank you. That means more than you know."

As the day waned, Edward and Clara prepared to leave. The flowers Clara had brought now sat in a vase on the kitchen table, their bright colors a reminder of the vibrant family ties that had grown stronger over the years.

"I'll keep you updated on James and Susan," Clara said as she hugged John tightly. "The next time we visit, there might be a little one in tow."

"And Nichole's wedding," Edward added. "You'll be there, of course."

John smiled, the warmth of their visit lingering. "Wouldn't miss it for the world."

As their car pulled out of the driveway, John stood on the porch, watching until it disappeared down the road. The silence of the house greeted him when he stepped back inside, but it felt less daunting now.

Angelica's presence was still there—in the flowers, in the echoes of laughter, and in the quiet love that had filled the day.

He looked at the vase of flowers, his smile soft. "You were right, Angelica. They're here because they care. And maybe... maybe I needed to be reminded of that."

The evening light bathed the house in a golden glow, and for the first time in a while, John felt a renewed sense of connection—not just to Angelica's memory, but to the family she had left behind.

For Tomorrow: A Song Found

The storm outside had grown fierce, rain lashing against the windows and wind howling through the eaves of Jane's School. John Anderson made his way down the dim hallway, his cane tapping against the tile floor. The faint light filtering through the frosted windows flickered as the storm pressed against the old building, testing its resilience.

He paused outside the music room, the door slightly ajar as it had been earlier. Something drew him back—a quiet pull he couldn't explain. Slowly, he pushed the door open and stepped inside.

The room was quiet except for the faint rattle of the windows in their frames. The piano stood sentinel in the corner, its presence as steady and familiar as ever. The air was thick with the scent of aged wood and dust, mingling with the echoes of melodies long since played.

John moved toward the piano, his fingers brushing its surface. The keys were smooth and cool under his touch, and for a moment, he considered playing. But something sticking out from the storage space inside the bench caught his eye—the edge of a piece of paper, yellowed with age.

He opened the lid and picked it up carefully, his breath catching as he recognized Angelica's handwriting scrawled across the top: *For Tomorrow.*

The notes on the page were bold and fluid, each one written with precision and care. It was a melody he didn't recognize, unfinished but filled with promise.

John sank onto the bench, holding the sheet music like it was something fragile and sacred. "Angelica," he whispered, his voice trembling.

He could almost hear her voice as he stared at the notes, filled with the same energy and hope that had defined her. *Music is about what's possible, John,* she'd always said. *It's about creating something that will last longer than we will.*

He ran his fingers over the page, his eyes tracing the melody. It was both familiar and new, a fragment of her that had been waiting for him, hidden in this room all these years.

The storm raged on outside, thunder rumbling in the distance as John placed the sheet music on the piano's stand. His hands hovered over the keys, hesitant at first, before pressing down to play the opening notes.

The melody was soft and tentative, the gaps in the music leaving room for his own interpretation. He played slowly, each note carrying the weight of memory and longing.

As the tune unfolded, something shifted within him. The storm outside seemed to quiet, its roar muted by the gentle strains of Angelica's song.

When he finished, the last note lingered in the air before fading into the silence. John sat back, the music still echoing in his mind.

He picked up the sheet again, studying the unfinished lines. There was space here—space for something new, for something more.

"Maybe it's not finished yet," he murmured, his voice steady despite the tears glistening in his eyes.

The room seemed to agree, the faint rattle of the windows almost like an encouraging whisper.

John folded the sheet music carefully, tucking it into the pocket of his coat. He stood, his hand resting on the piano for a moment longer.

"This isn't goodbye, Angelica," he said softly. "It's just... for tomorrow."

As he left the room, the storm outside surged again, but it no longer felt like something to fear. It was a song of its own, full of change and possibility—just as Angelica had always believed.

Playgrounds Don't Laugh Anymore

The wind whistled softly through the skeletal branches of the two great maples that flanked Jane's School. John stood by the window in the main hallway, his hands resting on the sill as he gazed out at the playground. The glass was speckled with dust and rain streaks, softening the view like an old photograph.

The merry-go-round stood at the center of the yard, its faded paint peeling to reveal rusted metal beneath. It swayed slightly in the wind, creaking with each gust. The swings hung limp, their chains twisted and the once-bright rubber seats dulled by years of sun and neglect. The slide, once polished to a gleaming silver by countless small hands and laughing children, was tarnished and streaked with grime.

John exhaled, the breath fogging the glass.

His memories filled the silence, transporting him back to a time when the playground had been the heart of the school.

He could see it vividly: children swarming the merry-go-round, their laughter ringing out as they spun each other faster and faster, shouting challenges to see who could hang on the longest. He remembered Angelica sitting on a bench near the swings, her auburn hair catching the sunlight as she watched the students play, her laughter mingling with theirs.

A young Bobby Ferillo came to mind, his violin case abandoned on the grass as he raced across the yard, chasing a soccer ball with an intensity that belied his usual calm demeanor. Tom wasn't far behind, his shouts of encouragement mixing with his brother's determined grins.

And then there were the quieter moments: the children sitting beneath the maples in the autumn, their jackets zipped tight against the chill as they shared secrets and snacks. The way the leaves would crunch underfoot in October, adding a symphony of nature to the playful cacophony.

Now, the silence was deafening.

John opened the door and stepped outside, his cane clicking softly against the pavement as he approached the playground. He paused at the merry-go-round, his fingers brushing against the cold metal rail. It shifted slightly under his touch, letting out a high-pitched squeal that seemed to echo endlessly in the empty yard.

He turned to the swings, their chains rattling faintly in the breeze. How many children had pumped their legs, reaching for the sky with the unshakable belief that they could touch the clouds?

The slide stood forlorn, its ladder missing a rung. He remembered the squeals of delight as kids rushed to the top, pushing and jostling for their turn. It had been a symbol of joy, of unrestrained childhood energy. Now it was little more than a monument to what had been.

John sank onto a bench near the edge of the yard, leaning heavily on his cane. He looked out over the faded playground, his heart heavy with the weight of time.

"I promised you I'd keep it alive," he murmured, his voice carried away by the wind. "But look at it now."

The wind stirred the leaves on the ground, carrying with it faint echoes of laughter—ghosts of the past that seemed to linger, refusing to be forgotten.

John closed his eyes, letting the memories wash over him. He could almost hear Angelica's voice, clear and warm as she hummed a tune while the children played. *It's not the swings or the slides that matter, John. It's the joy they bring. The memories they hold.*

He opened his eyes, the playground coming back into focus. For all its rust and wear, it wasn't truly gone. It still stood, waiting for life to fill it once more.

Rising slowly, John placed a hand on the merry-go-round again, giving it a gentle push. It turned reluctantly, its creak both mournful and determined.

"Maybe it's not too late," he said softly, his gaze sweeping the yard. "Not for this place. Not for me."

With a final look, he turned away from the school, his cane tapping a steady rhythm on the pavement. Behind him, the swings on the playground swayed slightly in the wind, as if nodding in quiet agreement.

A Journey to Indiana

1988

The morning sun filtered through the lace curtains of John Anderson's modest home, casting soft patterns across the packed suitcase sitting by the door. John sat in his armchair, a cup of coffee in hand, staring at the case as though it might vanish if he looked away for too long.

He wasn't one for travel. For all his years, everything he needed—his life, his memories—had been firmly rooted in the familiar soil of his home state. But today, for the first time, he was leaving it behind, at least for a little while.

"Angelica," he murmured, setting his coffee down on the table beside him. "I hope you'd be proud of me for this."

The letter from Nichole's fiancé had been sitting on his desk for weeks, the words neat and earnest: *We'd be honored to have you at the wedding, Uncle John. It wouldn't feel right without you there.*

He hadn't replied immediately. The thought of leaving home, of traveling to a place he'd never been, felt daunting. But Angelica's voice, the memory of her steadfast encouragement, had lingered in his mind. *You're part of their lives, John. Be there for them.*

The train ride to Indiana was a new experience, the rhythmic clatter of the wheels against the tracks both soothing and unsettling. John sat by the window, his cane leaning against the seat beside him, watching the countryside roll by in a blur of greens and browns.

The train was full of chatter—families traveling together, couples sharing quiet conversations—but John kept to himself, his thoughts occupied by the journey ahead. He had never been one to venture far from the places he knew, but something about this trip felt important.

A young man seated across from him broke into his thoughts. "First time on a train?"

John glanced up, startled. The man was in his twenties, dressed casually but neatly, a book open on his lap.

"First time out of my home state," John replied with a faint smile.

The man chuckled. "Big trip, then."

John nodded, his gaze shifting back to the window. "It's for my niece's wedding. Thought I might sit this one out, but... well, some things you just can't miss."

"Sounds like you made the right choice," the man said, his tone easy.

John didn't reply immediately, but the weight of the man's words settled over him like a quiet affirmation.

The station in Indiana was bustling, the air filled with the sound of announcements and the shuffle of travelers. John stepped off the train, his cane steadying him as he adjusted to the unfamiliar surroundings.

Edward and Clara were waiting for him near the entrance, their faces lighting up when they spotted him.

"John!" Edward called, waving.

Clara hurried forward, enveloping him in a warm hug. "You made it! How was the trip?"

"Long," John replied with a small smile. "But I'm here."

Edward clapped him on the shoulder, his grin wide. "Good to see you, John. Really good."

As they led him to the car, Clara chatted about the preparations for the wedding. The church, the flowers, the music—it was clear the event was a labor of love.

"Nichole's been over the moon," Clara said. "She can't wait for you to meet her fiancé's family. They've heard so much about you."

The church was small but beautiful, its wooden pews polished to a gleam. Nichole greeted John with an enthusiastic hug, her smile radiant.

"Uncle John! You're here!"

"Of course I am," he said, his voice warm. "Wouldn't miss it."

She introduced him to her fiancé, a kind-eyed young man named Aaron, and his family, who welcomed John with handshakes and warm smiles.

As the rehearsal unfolded, John found himself seated in a pew near the back, watching Nichole walk down the aisle with her father, her joy evident in every step.

It was a bittersweet moment. He thought of Angelica, of the way she would have adored this celebration. But instead of sadness, he felt a quiet pride—pride in Nichole, in the family Angelica had loved so deeply, and in himself for being part of it.

The day of the wedding dawned bright and clear, the Indiana sky a brilliant blue. John sat in the front row, his suit pressed, his cane resting at his side.

The ceremony was filled with laughter and tears, the vows heartfelt and sincere. As Nichole and Aaron exchanged rings, John couldn't help but think of his own wedding day, the way Angelica's smile had lit up the entire room.

When the reception began, John found himself seated at a table with Edward and Clara, the lively chatter of guests filling the hall.

Edward raised his glass, his voice carrying above the noise. "To Nichole and Aaron—a new beginning, and a reminder of all the love that brought us here."

John raised his glass as well, his gaze softening. "To Angelica," he said quietly, the words meant only for himself.

The train ride back felt quieter, the countryside a blur of green and gold in the late afternoon light. John leaned his head against the window, his thoughts filled with memories of the wedding.

It had been a journey unlike any he'd taken before, but it had reminded him of something Angelica had always known: love wasn't confined to one place. It was carried in the people who mattered, the connections that endured no matter how far life took you.

As the train pulled into the station back home, John stepped onto the platform with a renewed sense of purpose. He wasn't sure where life would take him next, but for now, he was content to let the journey unfold.

A Note and a Meeting

The note pinned to John Anderson's door was a simple scrap of lined paper, hastily folded and bearing Tom's familiar scrawl.

Mr. Anderson,

Emily Carter stopped by the district office today. She left word that she needs to meet with you ASAP. Said it was important. Thought you should know.

—Tom.

John read the note twice, his jaw tightening. His first reaction was irritation— Emily Carter had been dodging his calls and visits for months, as had everyone else at the district. Promises to make something of Jane's School had faded into polite deferrals, and now, three years after the closure, the building was still standing, its fate unresolved.

He tucked the note into his jacket pocket, sighing as he reached for his cane. "Urgent," he muttered to himself, the word leaving a sour taste. Nothing good ever came from "urgent" district matters.

The district office smelled of stale coffee and bureaucracy. John pushed open the heavy glass door, the cane in his right hand clicking against the tiled floor as he approached the reception desk.

"Mr. Anderson," the receptionist said, her tone polite but rehearsed. "Miss Carter is expecting you. Room 204, just down the hall."

He nodded, thanking her tersely as he made his way to the room. The hallway seemed longer than it had any right to be, each step echoing faintly.

When he entered Room 204, Emily Carter was already seated at a long table cluttered with papers and a steaming cup of coffee. She stood as he entered, her professional demeanor firmly in place.

"Mr. Anderson," she said, extending her hand.

John took it briefly, his grip firm. "Emily."

"Thank you for coming on short notice," she said, gesturing to the chair across from her. "Please, have a seat."

He sat, leaning his cane against the edge of the table. "Let's skip the pleasantries. What's this about?"

Emily hesitated, smoothing the front of her blazer before meeting his gaze. "It's about Jane's School."

John's brow furrowed. "Finally making a decision about it, are we?"

Emily nodded, her expression guarded. "Yes. The district has decided to sell the property."

John's jaw tightened, though he wasn't surprised. "Sell it to who?"

"There's interest from a few developers," Emily said carefully. "They're proposing residential housing or possibly a commercial space."

"Commercial space," John repeated, his tone sharp. "So, what? A strip mall? A chain grocery store?"

Emily's shoulders tensed. "I understand your frustration, but the district can't leave the building unused indefinitely. We've kept it on the books as long as we could, but…"

John leaned forward, his voice steady but firm. "You promised. You and everyone else promised that the school would be repurposed for the community. A center, a library—something that honored what it stood for. And now you're telling me that promise meant nothing?"

Emily's gaze didn't waver, though her tone softened. "It wasn't an easy decision, John. The funds from the sale will go toward improving educational resources for the district. It's not ideal, but it's practical."

"Practical," John said bitterly. "That's all it ever comes down to, isn't it?"

The room fell silent for a moment, the weight of the conversation pressing down on both of them.

"I didn't want you to hear this from anyone else," Emily said finally. "I know what the school meant to you, to the town. That's why I called this meeting."

John sat back, his grip tightening on the cane. "If you think I'm going to sit quietly and let this happen, you don't know me very well."

"I wouldn't expect you to," Emily replied, her tone even. "But I asked you to come here today for another reason as well. The district board has asked me to oversee the transition, and I want your help."

John blinked, caught off guard. "My help? Doing what? Holding the door open for the wrecking crew?"

Emily's expression didn't change. "The board values your insight, and so do I. You could have a say in how the process unfolds. Maybe even help ensure that part of the school's legacy is preserved."

John studied her for a long moment, his gaze sharp. "And why should I trust the district to do right by Jane's School now, after three years of nothing but broken promises?"

"Because I trust you," Emily said simply. "And because I know that if anyone can fight for the school's legacy, it's you."

The room fell quiet again, the tension thick but not unkind.

John sighed, leaning on his cane as he rose from the chair. "I'll think about it, Emily. But don't hold your breath."

"Thank you," she said, standing as well. "That's all I can ask."

As he turned to leave, Emily's voice stopped him. "Mr. Anderson?"

He looked back, his expression wary.

"For what it's worth, I meant what I said three years ago. I admire what you did for that school. And I'm sorry we couldn't do better by you."

John nodded curtly, the words too little, too late.

But as he stepped out into the bright afternoon sunlight, the note from Tom still in his pocket, a flicker of determination stirred in his chest.

The school's story wasn't over—not yet.

Letting Go

John Anderson gripped the edge of his car door, his knuckles white, as he leaned heavily against the frame. His head hung low, the lines on his face deeper than usual, etched by years of fighting battles he knew he couldn't win.

The tears started quietly, welling up in his eyes as his chest tightened with the weight of it all. He clenched his jaw, willing them away, but the harder he tried to suppress them, the more they rose.

The school wasn't just a building to him. It was Angelica's laughter echoing through the music room, the soft notes of her piano drifting into the halls, the life they had built together. Losing it felt like losing her all over again.

"I can't do this anymore," he whispered to himself, his voice hoarse.

The sound of hurried footsteps cut through his despair, and he looked up just as Emily Carter came into view. Her blazer flapped in the breeze, her face flushed from running across the parking lot.

"John," she called out, her voice steady but tinged with urgency. "John, wait."

He straightened slightly, brushing a hand over his face in a futile attempt to mask his grief. "What is it now, Emily?" he asked, his voice rough and tired.

She stopped a few feet away, catching her breath. "I really did try, John," she said, her tone earnest. "I need you to know that. I tried to fight for the school, for its legacy. I'm sorry it wasn't enough."

Her words landed heavily between them, and for a moment, John just stared at her, his chest rising and falling in uneven breaths.

"Doesn't matter," he muttered, his voice cracking. "Nothing matters anymore."

Before she could respond, his shoulders shook, and the tears he'd been holding back finally broke free. A sob escaped him, raw and unbidden, and he turned away, ashamed of his vulnerability.

But Emily stepped closer, placing a firm hand on his arm to steady him. "John, it's okay," she said softly, her voice steady despite the emotion tightening her throat.

He tried to pull away, shaking his head. "It's not about the school anymore, Emily," he choked out. "It's Angelica. It's always been Angelica. Keeping that school alive... it was my way of keeping her alive. And now it's gone. She's gone."

Emily's grip on his arm tightened, her other hand moving to his shoulder to brace him. "She's not gone, John," she said gently. "She's with you. In every life you touched together, in every note of music, in every leaf that falls from those maples. She's still here."

He leaned heavily against her, his sobs quieting but his breaths still uneven. "I don't know how to let go," he admitted, his voice barely audible.

"You don't have to let go of her," Emily said, her tone firm but kind. "Letting go of the school doesn't mean letting go of her. It just means carrying her memory in a different way."

John exhaled deeply, his hands gripping the cool metal of the car door as he steadied himself. He pulled back slightly, his eyes red but clearer now as he met Emily's gaze.

"I fought so hard," he said, his voice quieter now. "But maybe... maybe it's time to stop fighting."

Emily nodded, her expression a mix of sympathy and respect. "There's no shame in that, John. You've done more for that school—and this town—than anyone else ever could. It's okay to rest now."

He straightened slowly, brushing a hand over his face again as he drew in a long, steadying breath. "Rest," he repeated, the word heavy with meaning.

Emily stepped back, giving him space but watching him carefully. "If you ever need anything—anything at all—you know where to find me."

He gave a faint nod, the hint of a smile tugging at the corners of his lips. "Thank you, Emily. For everything."

She smiled softly, a mixture of relief and respect in her expression. "Take care, John."

As she turned and walked back toward the district office, John stood alone by his car, the cool breeze brushing against his face. The ache in his chest was still there, but it felt lighter now, less like a burden and more like a part of him he could carry forward.

He looked up at the sky, the clouds parting to reveal a stretch of pale blue. For the first time in a long while, he felt a glimmer of peace.

"Angelica," he murmured, his voice steady. "I think I'm ready."

With a deep breath, he climbed into the car and started the engine, the sound breaking the quiet of the parking lot. As he drove away, he didn't look back. The road ahead felt daunting, but it was his to forge.

One Last Walk Through Time

The rain had stopped entirely by the time John Anderson arrived at Jane's School. The sky was a steel gray, the kind of color that made spring flowers seem even brighter against their muted backdrop. The grass around the building was overgrown, dandelions and clover sprouting where the neat lawn used to be.

John parked his old sedan near the flagpole, now rusted and bare. He stepped out slowly, leaning on his cane as he surveyed the building. The windows were dark, the playground silent. Jane's School, which had once echoed with the sounds of children's laughter, stood like a forgotten relic.

He took a deep breath, adjusted his hat, and walked toward the doors.

Inside, the air was damp and musty, carrying a faint trace of chalk and old varnish. Tom Ferillo was waiting for him near the front hallway, a flashlight in hand.

"Evening, Mr. Anderson," Tom said, his voice subdued.

"Evening, Tom," John replied.

"You sure about this?" Tom asked, his keys jangling softly as he gestured toward the shadowy halls.

"I am," John said, his tone resolute. "One last walk."

They moved through the library first, its shelves now completely empty. Dust motes danced in the flashlight's beam as Tom swung it around the room.

"Remember the reading contests Angelique used to run?" John said, his voice carrying a hint of warmth. "She'd bribe the kids with lollipops, and they'd devour books just to get them."

Tom chuckled, running his fingers along a bare shelf. "She got me once. I read that whole Boxcar Children book for a cherry sucker."

John smiled faintly, his gaze lingering on the corner where Angelique's desk had once stood. "She had a way of making people feel like they could do anything."

In the science lab, the faint smell of chemicals lingered, though the tables and cabinets were bare.

"This is where I failed my first chemistry test," Tom admitted, his laugh quiet but genuine.

"And where you built the best baking soda volcano this school ever saw," John countered, his eyes twinkling.

Tom shrugged, his grin sheepish. "Had to make up for the test somehow."

John rested a hand on one of the tables, his fingers tracing its worn surface. "This place wasn't just about teaching facts. It was about discovery. Wonder. Every child who sat here left with something they didn't have before."

The gymnasium felt cavernous now, its echoes amplified in the emptiness. The farewell banner still hung above the stage, though its edges were frayed, and the letters had begun to fade.

"This room held everything," John said, his voice soft. "Concerts, assemblies, dances. It was the heartbeat of the school."

Tom walked to the center of the gym, his footsteps loud against the wood. "I remember Bobby's first recital here. The whole town showed up."

John's chest tightened at the memory. "He was nervous that night. Angelica sat with him backstage, held his hand until it was his turn."

"She was good at that," Tom said quietly. "Making people brave."

John nodded, his gaze fixed on the banner. "She always said this room could hold the weight of the world."

They returned to the front hallway, the lockers standing like silent sentinels.

Tom handed John the keys, his expression somber. "You want to do the honors?"

John stared at the padlock on the double doors, the same lock he had turned so many times before. His hand trembled slightly as he reached out, fitting the key into the lock.

The click of the padlock echoed in the quiet hallway.

John stepped back, his gaze sweeping the space one final time. "It's not the walls or the roof that made this place special," he said. "It's the people who filled it with life."

Tom placed a hand on John's shoulder. "You kept it alive as long as you could. Longer than anyone else would have."

John smiled faintly, his eyes glistening. "I did my best. That's all Angelica ever asked for."

Outside, the air was crisp and fresh, the rain having washed the world clean. The maples swayed gently in the breeze, their branches full of new leaves.

Tom turned to John as they stood near the car. "What's next for you?"

John looked up at the sky, the gray clouds parting to reveal patches of blue. For the first time in a long while, he felt the weight of the past lift slightly.

"I'll find something," he said simply. "Something to carry this forward. It's what she would've wanted."

Tom smiled, his respect clear. "You'll find it, Mr. Anderson. You always do."

They shook hands, and as Tom walked toward his truck, John lingered by the maples, their leaves rustling softly.

"I'll keep my promise," he murmured, his voice steady. "For you, Angelica. Always."

Pot Roast and New Beginnings

Tom leaned against the hood of his old truck, his hands tucked into his jacket pockets. He glanced over at John, who stood a few steps away, his cane in one hand and the other resting on the roof of his car.

"You know," Tom began, breaking the silence, "I don't think you should spend the night alone after all this."

John turned toward him, raising an eyebrow. "And what would you suggest?"

Tom smiled faintly, tilting his head toward the truck. "Come by my place. Cindy's been asking about you. The kids, too. They've heard all about 'Mr. Anderson, the school's heart and soul.' Thought it might be nice for them to finally meet the man behind the legend."

John chuckled softly, shaking his head. "A legend, am I? Not sure I'd go that far."

"Don't sell yourself short," Tom replied. "This town doesn't have a lot of legends, but you? You're one of 'em. Besides, Cindy makes a mean pot roast. You'd be doing me a favor—less leftovers for me to eat for lunch all week."

John hesitated, his gaze drifting back toward the school. Its silhouette was stark against the night sky, the windows dark and the doors locked. The weight of the evening pressed on him, but Tom's offer felt like a light cutting through the haze.

"You're sure it wouldn't be an imposition?" John asked, his tone cautious but curious.

Tom shook his head. "Not in the slightest. You're family, Mr. Anderson. Always have been."

The words settled over John like a warm blanket, easing the ache in his chest.

"I'd like that," he said quietly.

Tom's smile widened, and he pushed off the truck. "Great. Follow me. It's just a ten-minute drive—less if you can keep up."

John chuckled again, feeling lighter than he had in weeks. "We'll see about that."

As they climbed into their vehicles, the rain began to fall again, soft and gentle this time. The sound of it on the car roof was soothing as John started the engine and pulled out of the parking lot behind Tom's truck.

For the first time in a long while, he felt a sense of connection—a reminder that even as one chapter of his life closed, there were still new relationships and moments waiting for him.

The school was gone, but the spirit of its community remained, carried forward by people like Tom, Cindy, and their children.

And as John followed Tom's taillights through the quiet streets, he realized that the end of one era didn't have to mean the end of everything. Sometimes, it simply marked the beginning of something new.

Around the Lake and to the Table

The rain started again, falling in a steady rhythm against the windshield as John Anderson guided his car along the winding road that curved around the lake. The water stretched out beside him, a vast expanse of dark ripples glistening faintly under the occasional streetlamp.

Angelica had always loved storms, and for a moment, he could almost hear her voice. *"It's the chaos of it,"* she used to say, her smile wide and her eyes alight. *"It shakes everything loose, leaves you clearer when it's gone."*

The car heater hummed softly, filling the quiet space as John's thoughts drifted.

He remembered the countless drives they had taken together, Angelica's hand resting lightly on his arm as she gazed out at the water. She would hum melodies to herself, sometimes breaking into full songs when the mood struck her.

Storms had never unnerved her; they had inspired her.

"She saw beauty in things falling apart," John murmured, his fingers tightening briefly on the steering wheel.

The road curved, and his headlights illuminated a cluster of cattails swaying in the breeze near the shoreline.

For the first time since the school's closure became inevitable, John felt that same clarity Angelica had spoken of. The storm—both outside and within—was clearing. He wasn't leaving everything behind. He was carrying it forward, reshaping it into something that could endure.

By the time he reached Tom's house, the rain had lessened to a drizzle. The modest two-story home glowed warmly from within, the windows alive with light.

Tom was waiting on the front porch, hands on his hips, his grin visible even in the dim light.

"Thought you got lost," he teased as John parked in the driveway.

"Just taking the scenic route," John replied as he stepped out, grabbing his cane.

"Well, you're right on time. Cindy's been keeping the roast warm, and the kids are ready to pounce the second you walk in the door."

John chuckled softly as he followed Tom up the steps and into the house.

Inside, the scent of home-cooked food filled the air—rich and savory, with a hint of something sweet. The living room was cozy, scattered with evidence of family life: toys tucked into a corner, a stack of magazines on the coffee table, and a quilt draped over the back of the couch.

"Mr. Anderson!" a young voice called out, and two children came bounding into the room—a boy and a girl, both under ten, their faces alight with excitement.

"Now, what did I tell you about running in the house?" Cindy's voice followed them, warm but firm as she emerged from the kitchen, wiping her hands on a dish towel.

She smiled when she saw John, her face kind and welcoming. "You must be starving. Come on, everything's ready."

Dinner was served in the small dining room, the table crowded with dishes: a steaming pot roast surrounded by carrots and potatoes, a bowl of buttery rolls, and a plate of green beans. The children chattered excitedly, asking John questions about the school and his time as principal.

"Is it true you let my dad's brother, Bobby, play the piano every day after class?" the boy asked, his eyes wide.

John smiled, nodding. "It's true. He was one of the most talented students I ever met. Your dad used to tag along sometimes, didn't you, Tom?"

Tom, busy helping his daughter cut her meat, laughed. "I tried, but I was no Bobby."

"You had other gifts," John said, his tone gentle but firm.

Cindy chimed in. "And now he's teaching the kids how to fix everything under the sun. I'd say that's a gift."

The conversation flowed easily as the meal went on. Cindy shared stories about the children, Tom recounted memories from his own school days, and the kids hung on every word John said, their enthusiasm infectious.

For John, it was a reminder of why Jane's School had meant so much. It wasn't just the building or the lessons—it was the connections, the way it brought people together, creating bonds that lasted long after the last bell rang.

As the evening wound down, John found himself sitting on the couch with a cup of coffee, the children curled up under the quilt beside him, listening intently as he told them a story about Angelica's first concert at the school.

"She made everyone believe in the power of music," he said, his voice soft with memory. "And in themselves."

Cindy leaned against the doorframe, her arms crossed as she watched the scene with a warm smile. Tom sat in an armchair, his gaze thoughtful.

"You're welcome here anytime, Mr. Anderson," Tom said finally, his voice steady.

John nodded, his chest full in a way he hadn't felt in years. "Thank you, Tom. I think I'll take you up on that."

As the rain continued to patter gently against the windows, John felt something he hadn't expected to find tonight: a sense of home.

It wasn't tied to a building or a job—it was here, in the connections that had carried him through the years and the new ones forming even now.

A Sky Washed Clean

The rain had stopped almost entirely by the time John Anderson pulled out of Tom's driveway, the gentle patter against his windshield replaced by a stillness that felt almost sacred. His wipers made a final sweep across the glass before he turned them off, leaving the quiet hum of the engine and the faint rustling of the breeze as his only companions.

The streets were slick and black, reflecting the glow of the streetlights in wavering pools. The air outside was crisp and clean, carrying with it the unmistakable scent of rain-soaked earth and fallen leaves. As John drove, his thoughts drifted, carried by the calm that followed the storm.

The town seemed different tonight, quieter, more peaceful. It wasn't just the absence of the storm—it was as if the tension that had gripped John's heart for so long had finally begun to loosen.

He turned onto the winding road that followed the lake's edge, the headlights of his car casting long, shimmering reflections on the water. The lake stretched out like a vast mirror, its surface broken only by the occasional ripple from the gentle breeze.

Angelica had always loved this stretch of road.

"Let's stop," she used to say, her excitement bubbling over like a child's. *"Just for a moment. The lake's too beautiful to rush past."*

Without hesitation, John slowed the car, pulling onto the shoulder at a familiar overlook. He turned off the engine, plunging the car into darkness save for the soft glow of the moonlight.

Stepping out, he leaned on his cane as he made his way to the edge of the embankment. The air was cool, wrapping around him in a way that was both bracing and comforting. The storm clouds had cleared completely, leaving a sky scattered with stars.

The lake mirrored the heavens, each ripple catching the faint light and scattering it like fragments of a dream.

John stood there for a long moment, his thoughts quiet but steady.

The storm had raged tonight, as storms always did. Fierce, unyielding, it had seemed intent on tearing the world apart. But now, in the stillness that followed, John could see what Angelica had always meant.

"Storms are nature's way of clearing things out," she'd told him during a drive like this one, years ago. *"They shake loose what's broken and leave room for what's new to grow. They're not something to fear, John. They're something to embrace."*

He had resisted that lesson for so long, clinging to what he thought he couldn't lose: the school, the routines, even the grief that had tethered him to Angelica. But now, as he stood by the lake, he understood.

The storm didn't destroy—it transformed.

The wind picked up briefly, rustling the trees along the embankment. John closed his eyes, letting the sound wash over him. He could almost hear Angelica's laughter in the breeze, her voice warm and full of life.

"Thank you," he whispered, the words carried off into the night.

When he opened his eyes, the lake seemed to shimmer more brightly, as if acknowledging his gratitude. He smiled faintly, the weight on his chest lifting like a fog burned away by the morning sun.

Back in the car, John turned onto the narrow road leading home. The headlights illuminated the familiar shapes of the trees lining the driveway, their wet branches glistening like polished silver.

He parked in the gravel lot in front of the house, the engine's rumble fading into the quiet as he stepped out. The house loomed ahead, its windows dark but welcoming. The porch light glowed faintly, casting a golden halo over the front steps.

John paused before going inside, his gaze drifting to the garden Angelica had tended with such care. Even in the dim light, he could see the remnants of her touch—the stubborn perennials that survived every winter, the stone path she'd laid with her own hands.

Inside, the house felt less empty than it had in years. The storm's passing had left something behind—a stillness that wasn't lonely, but peaceful.

John shrugged off his coat and hung it on the familiar hook by the door. He placed his cane by the umbrella stand, his movements unhurried.

The living room beckoned, its quiet warmth drawing him toward the piano. The instrument sat by the window, its polished surface reflecting the moonlight.

He approached it slowly, sitting on the bench with a sense of purpose. The sheet music he'd found earlier—*For Tomorrow*—was still tucked into his coat pocket. He retrieved it, smoothing the edges carefully before placing it on the stand.

For a moment, he simply sat there, his fingers resting lightly on the keys. The silence in the house was complete, save for the faint ticking of the clock on the mantel.

Then he began to play.

The melody was tentative at first, his hands rediscovering the flow of the notes. But as the song unfolded, it grew stronger, more confident. It wasn't just Angelica's music anymore—it was his, too.

The storm had left its mark, but so had the calm.

As the final note faded into the quiet, John looked out the window. The stars were brighter now, the sky vast and open, and for the first time in a long while, he felt ready to move forward.

Not by leaving everything behind, but by carrying it with him, like the melody of Angelica's song.

The storm had cleared, and so had he.

Roots in Her Honor

1989

The morning air was crisp and full of promise, the sunlight breaking through the retreating clouds to bathe the world in golden light. The storm had left the earth soft and damp, the perfect condition for planting.

John Anderson stood in his backyard, a small sapling cradled in his hands. Its thin trunk and delicate branches trembled slightly in the breeze, but the roots were strong, wrapped in dark, rich soil.

The sapling was an oak, chosen not for its speed of growth but for its endurance. It was the kind of tree that would stand tall through countless storms, its roots digging deep, its branches reaching skyward with unshakable resolve.

John had thought long and hard about this moment. The idea had come to him the night before, as he sat at the piano, Angelica's unfinished melody still echoing in his mind. She had always believed in creating things that lasted—songs, traditions, connections.

Planting this tree felt right. It was a gesture, small but meaningful, that tied the past to the future.

With his shovel in hand, John moved to the spot he'd chosen near the garden Angelica had loved so much. It was a place where the sun lingered longest in the afternoon, where flowers would bloom in the spring and birds might rest in the branches as the tree grew.

He dug the hole slowly, the rhythm of the shovel against the earth steady and deliberate. The rich smell of soil filled the air as he worked, his breaths coming evenly despite the occasional ache in his back.

When the hole was ready, John carefully placed the sapling inside, spreading its roots gently. He knelt beside it, his hands firm but gentle as he adjusted the soil around the base.

"There you go," he said softly, his voice carrying a hint of the affection he'd once spoken to Angelica with. "This is your home now."

As he tamped the earth down, his mind filled with images of the tree's future.

He imagined its roots spreading deep into the soil, anchoring it firmly as it weathered its first winters. He saw its branches growing thick and strong, providing shade in the heat of summer and catching the golden light of autumn.

And in the far-off years, when his own time had passed, he pictured others finding solace beneath its canopy—children playing, families gathering, strangers pausing to rest.

The tree would stand as a testament to resilience and growth, just as Angelica had been in life.

John stood, brushing the soil from his hands. The sapling looked small and fragile, but it held an unspoken promise.

He stepped back, resting a hand on his cane as he admired his work.

"You always said we should plant things for tomorrow," he murmured, his gaze lifting to the sky. "I think you'd like this one, Angelica."

He stayed there for a long moment, letting the warmth of the sun wash over him. The sapling swayed gently in the breeze, its leaves rustling faintly, almost like a song.

As John turned to head back toward the house, he felt a sense of peace settle over him. The tree wasn't just a memorial—it was a new beginning, a living reminder of the love and legacy he and Angelica had shared.

It would grow with the seasons, changing but enduring, just as their memories would.

And as John glanced back at the sapling one last time, a small smile played at his lips.

This was a future Angelica would have believed in.

Dear Angelica...

The early evening sun dipped low on the horizon, casting a warm, amber glow over John Anderson's small study. The room smelled faintly of cedar and aged paper, the quiet hum of the world outside broken only by the scratch of John's pen against paper.

The desk was cluttered but purposeful: a neat stack of blank sheets, a few envelopes, and a coffee mug bearing the faded logo of Jane's School. Beside it rested the sapling's planting trowel, cleaned but still showing faint streaks of dirt—a reminder of the morning's work.

John leaned back in his chair, reading over the letter he had begun. His handwriting was deliberate, each stroke of the pen carrying a quiet weight.

Dear Angelica,

Today, I planted a tree for you. It's just a sapling now, barely taller than my knee, but I can see what it will become. Strong. Resilient. A place for others to find rest and comfort. I think you'd like it. It stands by your garden— your favorite spot—and it feels like you're still here with me somehow.

This storm we had—it reminded me of the things you always tried to teach me. About change. About letting go. And more importantly, about embracing what comes after. I think I'm finally starting to understand, Angelica. You were always ahead of me in that way.

John paused, his gaze drifting to the window. Outside, the sapling stood quietly in the twilight, its small leaves rustling in the evening breeze. He smiled faintly, tapping the pen against the edge of the desk before leaning forward again.

I've decided to take on something new. Something that feels a little daunting, but I think you'd be proud. The library board offered me a position, Angelica. They want me to help expand programs for kids and families—to bring some of what we loved about Jane's School into the community's heart. And you know what? I said yes.
I can already hear you laughing at my hesitation. "Of course, you'll say yes, John," you'd tell me. "Who else would they trust with something so important?" I suppose you'd be right, as usual.

John chuckled softly at his own words, shaking his head as he dipped the pen back into the inkwell.

The librarian, Angelique—you remember her, don't you?—has been full of ideas already. Story hours, music programs, even a place for teens to hang out after school. She reminded me of you today, talking with that same fire in her eyes. I think you would've gotten along just fine.

I'll admit, it's strange to start something new at my age. I spent so many years thinking Jane's School was the only place where I belonged. But now I see that it wasn't just the building. It was the people. The connections. And those don't end, Angelica. They just find new forms, new homes.

The pen paused as John leaned back, gazing at the growing twilight outside. A single star twinkled faintly in the sky, a promise of the night to come.

He let out a slow breath and turned back to the letter.

I wish you could see this town, Angelica. Even in change, it's still full of the same life and spirit that you loved. And I'll be here to keep that spirit alive, in whatever way I can. This isn't a goodbye to what we built together—it's a continuation.

Tomorrow, I'll meet with Angelique and the rest of the board to discuss our plans. Maybe I'll bring along a little of your music, just for inspiration. I think the children could use a song like "For Tomorrow."

I miss you, Angelica. Every day. But I feel you here, in the trees, in the music, and now, in this new purpose. Thank you for everything you gave me—for showing me how to grow, even now.

John placed the pen down gently, folding the letter with care. He slid it into an envelope, sealing it with quiet deliberation before tucking it into a wooden box on the desk.

The box was an old one, its edges worn smooth with time, but it still bore the faint traces of Angelica's initials carved into the lid. It had once held her favorite sheet music; now, it would hold his letters to her.

He stood, stretching slightly, and walked to the window. The sapling stood tall in the fading light, its presence steady and full of quiet promise.

"Tomorrow," he said softly, his voice carrying the weight of hope and renewal.

For now, there were no bells ringing, no students filling the halls. But there were still stories to tell, lessons to share, and roots to plant.

And John knew he was exactly where he was meant to be.

Pirates, Roast Chicken, and Family Feels

The sound of children laughing drifted through the open window as John Anderson pulled into Tom and Cindy Ferillo's driveway. The warm glow of their home spilled out onto the yard, where the two Ferillo children were chasing each other with toy swords. Their playful shouts carried a cheerful chaos that reminded John of the school playground in its heyday.

He stepped out of the car, leaning on his cane as he walked toward the house. Tom emerged from the porch, waving enthusiastically.

"Mr. Anderson! You're just in time!" Tom called, his grin wide.

"For what, exactly?" John asked, raising an eyebrow but smiling all the same.

"Dad says we're having a pirate duel!" shouted Tom's son, his plastic sword raised high.

"And the loser does the dishes!" added the daughter, giggling as she darted behind her brother.

"Don't let them rope you into this one, Mr. Anderson," Tom said, shaking his head. "They'll claim a win no matter what."

John chuckled as he stepped onto the porch. "I'll leave the swordplay to the experts. Besides, I'm here for the food and the company."

Cindy appeared at the door, wiping her hands on a kitchen towel. "And you'll get plenty of both," she said warmly. "Come on in—it's a little loud, but it's home."

Inside, the house was alive with the kind of comforting clutter that came with family life. The dining table was set for five, its center adorned with a bouquet of flowers that looked freshly picked. A faint aroma of roasted chicken and herbs filled the air, mingling with the sweetness of freshly baked bread.

John felt an immediate sense of belonging as he shrugged off his coat and hung it on the familiar hook by the door.

"You've been busy," he said, nodding toward the colorful artwork taped to the fridge.

"Mom said I could draw a pirate map," Tom's daughter chimed in, beaming. "Wanna see?"

"Of course," John replied, leaning slightly as she rushed to retrieve her masterpiece.

As the family settled around the table, the clatter of dishes and the hum of conversation created a warmth that wrapped around John like a favorite old coat. The children chatted excitedly, filling the space with stories about school, imaginary adventures, and their plans for the weekend.

Tom and Cindy exchanged amused glances as they passed dishes of food around, their teamwork so seamless it was as if they could read each other's minds.

"And how's the library board going?" Cindy asked, her voice cutting through the cheerful din.

John smiled. "Busy, but in a good way. We're starting to put some programs in place—story hours for the little ones, a music circle inspired by Angelica's teaching. It feels... meaningful."

Cindy reached across the table, giving his hand a squeeze. "She'd be so proud of you."

After dinner, the children pulled John into the living room for a game of cards. It was a simple affair, full of laughter and playful accusations of cheating, and for John, it felt like slipping back into a world he hadn't realized he missed so much.

Tom sat on the couch, watching his kids and their "adopted grandfather" with a quiet smile. "You know, Mr. Anderson, you're really part of the family now. The kids already think of you that way."

John glanced up, his heart swelling. "It feels good. Being here, with all of you— it feels right."

Later, as he prepared to leave, Cindy handed him a small tin wrapped in a checkered cloth. "Some leftovers for tomorrow," she said with a wink.

"You spoil me, Cindy," John said, his tone light but sincere.

"Not at all," she replied. "We're just glad to have you here."

Outside, the air was cool, carrying the faint scent of woodsmoke from a neighbor's fireplace. John paused by his car, looking back at the house as the family waved goodbye from the porch.

As he drove home, the warmth of the evening lingered, filling him with a quiet joy.

Tom and Cindy weren't just friends—they were becoming his family.

"It does feel good," he said softly to himself, smiling as the stars guided him home.

Autumn's Gentle Goodbye

1990

The crisp autumn air greeted John Anderson as he stepped onto the grounds of Jane's School. The familiar scent of fallen leaves and damp earth carried with it a flood of memories, but instead of the ache he had come to expect, there was something else—peace.

The path leading to the school was carpeted in vibrant hues of red, orange, and gold, each step crunching softly beneath his worn shoes. The two great maples stood tall as ever, their branches swaying gently in the breeze. Their leaves fluttered to the ground in a slow, deliberate dance, as if the trees themselves were paying homage to the passage of time.

John paused at the edge of the schoolyard, his cane steadying him as he surveyed the place that had been the center of his life for more than four decades. The building, though quiet and closed, seemed less forlorn today. It felt timeless, enduring—like the maples.

He walked slowly toward the flagpole, the central walkway etched into his memory. He remembered every detail of it: the sound of children's feet running toward the playground, Angelica's voice rising above the chatter as she called students inside, the distant squeak of the merry-go-round on windy days.

As he reached the base of the flagpole, he rested his hand on its cool metal. For years, this had been the school's anchor, Angelica's so-called "compass," pointing the way for generations of students. Now, it stood empty, but its symbolism felt no less significant.

John looked up at the sky, the crisp blue stretching endlessly above.

"It's been a year," he said aloud, his voice quiet but firm.

The words weren't meant for anyone in particular, yet they seemed to settle into the space around him, grounding him.

His eyes shifted to the playground, the swings hanging still, their chains slightly rusted. The merry-go-round bore its age in peeling paint and patches of exposed metal, but it stood steady, just as it always had.

He could see the echoes of the past there: children laughing, chasing each other in games that only made sense to them. Bobby and Tom playing soccer, their sibling rivalry spilling over in playful shouts. Angelica sitting on the bench near the swings, her hands clasped around a mug of coffee as she watched the students with a mixture of pride and amusement.

The memories warmed him. They weren't ghosts, haunting him with what he had lost—they were a testament to what had been, and what would always be.

John turned his attention back to the maples, their towering forms vibrant against the backdrop of the clear autumn sky. Their roots had withstood countless storms, their branches bending but never breaking.

The trees had taught him something profound: resilience wasn't about resisting change—it was about adapting, growing stronger, and finding new ways to thrive.

He thought of the sapling he had planted in Angelica's memory, now growing in his yard. It was young, still finding its place in the world, but its roots were strong. Just like the roots of this place, and the legacy it had built.

John moved to the bench beneath one of the maples, easing himself down with a sigh. He rested his cane beside him, leaning back to take in the scene.

His thoughts turned to the year that had passed. The closure of the school had been difficult, but it had led him to new beginnings. The library board had given him a purpose—bringing story hours, music programs, and community events to life.

He thought of Angelica's melody, *For Tomorrow*, now a favorite at the library's children's programs. He thought of Tom, Cindy, and their kids, who had become his family in ways he hadn't expected.

Most of all, he thought of the letters he'd written to Angelica—letters that had helped him process his grief and rediscover his joy.

The wind picked up, rustling the leaves overhead and scattering a handful of them at John's feet. One in particular caught his eye—a brilliant red leaf, its edges outlined in gold. He picked it up, turning it over in his hands.

The leaf was fleeting, its beauty lasting only for a season, but its purpose was clear. It would nourish the soil, paving the way for new growth when spring arrived.

"That's what you always said, Angelica," he murmured, a small smile tugging at his lips. "The end of one thing is just the beginning of something else."

As the afternoon light began to fade, John rose from the bench, his cane steady in his hand. He turned to face the school one last time, its windows dark but its presence strong.

"Thank you," he said softly, his voice filled with gratitude and closure.

The maples swayed gently in the breeze, their branches seeming to nod in acknowledgment.

John made his way back down the path, his steps sure and steady. The town awaited him, alive with the rhythms of community he had come to cherish.

He knew he would return to this place—next autumn, and the one after that. Not out of longing, but out of love.

The school was more than bricks and mortar. Its legacy lived in him, in the community, in every life it had touched.

And as the leaves crunched beneath his feet, John felt ready to embrace whatever the next season would bring.

This was a new autumn—not an end, but a beginning.

The drive home was quiet, the hum of the engine and the rhythmic swish of the windshield wipers the only sounds. The sun had dipped below the horizon, leaving the sky painted in deep purples and blues. John gripped the steering wheel with steady hands, the image of Jane's School fading into the rearview mirror.

The day had been heavy, but not in the way it used to be. The weight of loss had softened into something quieter, less jagged. The maples' gentle goodbye had felt final in its way, but it hadn't closed the door on the past. It had simply reminded him that he could carry it with him into the future.

When John pulled into his driveway, the porch light cast a warm glow over the familiar contours of his home. The sapling he had planted in Angelica's memory swayed gently in the cool evening breeze, its leaves catching the light like tiny lanterns.

He stepped inside, hanging his coat on the rack and placing his cane by the door. The house greeted him with its usual stillness, a kind of quiet he had grown accustomed to over the years but still hadn't entirely made peace with.

Later, as he prepared for bed, John sat on the edge of the mattress, slipping off his shoes with a practiced ease. He reached for the small drawer in the nightstand, searching for his reading glasses, but his fingers met only empty space.

He frowned, leaning over to look under the bed where they must have fallen. Sure enough, the glasses lay just out of reach, their thin frames glinting faintly in the dim light of the bedside lamp.

With a sigh, he lowered himself onto the floor, his joints protesting the movement. Propping himself on one arm, he stretched toward the glasses but couldn't quite grasp them.

"Always just beyond reach," he muttered to himself.

Pushing the nightstand aside for better access, he froze mid-motion. Tucked against the baseboard was an envelope, yellowed with age and slightly crumpled.

John's breath caught as he saw his name written on the front in Angelica's familiar handwriting.

For a moment, he didn't move, his heart pounding in his chest. Slowly, carefully, he picked up the envelope, his fingers trembling.

"Angelica," he whispered.

The envelope was sealed but brittle from the years. He sat back on the bed, the reading glasses forgotten, and carefully opened it. Inside was a single sheet of paper, folded neatly.

As he unfolded it, her handwriting greeted him—strong, flowing, unmistakably hers.

My dearest John,

If you're reading this, it means you've come home, and I'm no longer there to welcome you. I hope you found this when you needed it most, though I wish I could be there to say these things to you in person.

You've always been my rock, my steady hand, my North Star. But even rocks need time to rest, and stars sometimes need to shine alone to light their way. You've given so much of yourself—to me, to the school, to this town—and I've seen how it's weighed on you. You've carried it all with grace, but, my love, you don't have to carry it forever.

I want you to live, John. Not just for me, not just for the school—but for yourself. There's so much of the world left for you to see, so many melodies left for you to hear. You've given your heart to everyone else for so long. Now, it's time to give some of it back to yourself.

When you think of me, don't let it bring you sorrow. Let it bring you joy, the way your love always brought it to me. I'll be with you in the music, in the rustling of the leaves, in every sunrise and sunset. I'll be with you, always.

And when you're ready, my love, let yourself dream of new beginnings. Because the best way to honor what we've built together is to keep building, to keep growing, to keep living.

Yours forever,

Angelica

John sat in the stillness of the room, the letter resting on his lap, Angelica's words settling over him like a warm embrace.

The tears came quietly, not from grief but from the profound sense of love her letter carried. Her words were not a goodbye—they were a call to carry forward, a reminder of everything they had shared and everything still ahead.

He looked over at the nightstand where a small photograph of Angelica stood, her smile as radiant as he remembered.

"You always knew what I needed to hear, didn't you?" he murmured, his voice thick with emotion.

Placing the letter carefully back into its envelope, John returned it to the nightstand, this time in a drawer where he could find it again. He pushed the furniture back into place and stood, his movements slow but steady.

As he turned off the bedside lamp and settled under the covers, a calm sense of purpose filled him. The maples, the school, the letters he had written—they were all part of the same story, and Angelica's letter was a new chapter he hadn't known he needed.

Tomorrow would come with its own challenges, but tonight, John let himself rest, his heart lighter than it had been in years.

Angelica had always been his guide, and now, even in her absence, she was leading him still.

Thank you for reading…

August
Rains

Songbird
IN THE
Rain
Robert Stanek

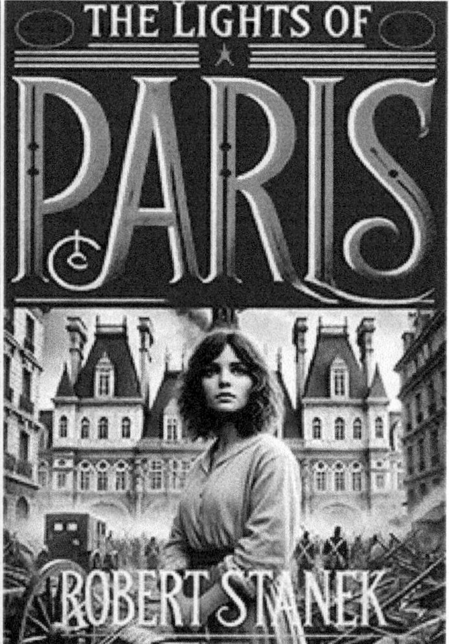

THE LIGHTS OF
PARIS
ROBERT STANEK

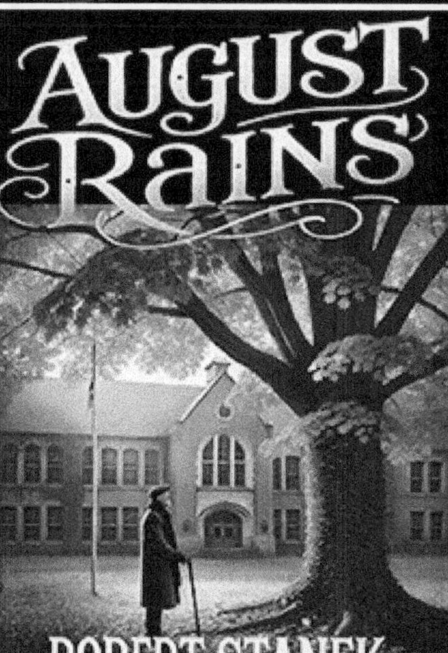

AUGUST
RAINS
ROBERT STANEK

ALMOST
CALIFORNIA
IGH SCHOOL
ROBERT STANEK

About the Author

Robert Stanek is a writer who loves exploring the quiet, transformative moments that define human lives. With a background in teaching and a passion for storytelling, Stanek crafts narratives that honor the resilience of everyday people and the legacies they leave behind.

August Rains grew out of a desire to reflect on the lasting influence of educators, mentors, and community members. Set against the backdrop of a changing world, the novel delves into themes of memory, love, and renewal.

When not writing, Robert Stanek enjoys wandering through autumn woods, finding inspiration in the changing seasons, and spending time with loved ones. You can connect with Robert Stanek on robert-stanek.com, where he shares updates on his work and insights into his creative process.

www.ingramcontent.com/pod-product-compliance
Lightning Source LLC
Chambersburg PA
CBHW060241100726
47907CB00003B/725